Dead Cats

AND OTHER REFLECTIONS ON PARENTHOOD

Jesse McKinnell

Thanks

Shine Box Publishing

Cover drawings by Forrest J. Stone (forjstone.com)

Cover and back design by Becky McKinnell (ibeccreative.com)

ISBN: 978-0-692-10185-8

For Becky, I promise to never be this.

CHAPTER ONE
Friskers

THE DEAD CAT is starting to smell. Ignoring the sour stench of death, I confidently hold its carcass up in front of the judge. The tabby's eyes bulge and stare back into mine. Under the table my left hand has gone from pins and needles to completely numb. I try shaking it to no effect. This is what happens when you use lidocaine recreationally.

"Your Honor, clearly the feline had expired prior to making contact with the undercarriage of my client's car."

My wife's constant sobbing is distracting.

Bill, my lawyer, continues making our case to the judge. "Your Honor, a close examination of the animal's abdomen shows no signs of bruising at the impact site where the tire made contact. Mr. Peterson, please rotate the cat so His Honor can take a closer look at the animal's stomach."

Holding the animal by the tail with my right hand, I raise it to face level, gingerly pinch the cat's ear, then turn it ninety degrees so the judge can see the tire marks.

"Please note, Your Honor, that although the torso has been flattened and the tires left considerable indentation in the ribs, there are no signs of bruising. Were the cat alive at the time of the accident, all the grooves left by the tire would have pooled with blood resulting in visible bruises. However, since the animal had expired previously, the blood had already congealed and *did not* flow to the site of the trauma, proving my client's contact with the animal to be posthumous." Bill pauses to let his point soak into the room.

"Now, if you'll review the pictures which have been included as exhibits to my client's response, you will find a close-up of the entrails which were evacuated out of the cat's mouth and anus." The stenographer's fingers whistled along the keyboard not missing a word of the brilliance spewing forth in my defense. "As you can plainly see, although there is plenty of gore, there is no blood."

Bill is lying of course, and I'm paying him good money to do it. Friskers absolutely died under the back tire of one of the finest automobiles ever crafted by man, a fate far better than the little orange turd deserved, but I don't think Bill knows he's committing perjury or whatever it's called when a lawyer lies to a judge. It's been hard to keep track of all the things that come out of my mouth. Life, lately, has had a way of getting hazy on me.

Bill Johnson is so fully lathered up now, worked into a state where the truth is almost beside the point. A small amount of spit gathers at the corners of his mouth as he spins this yarn for the judge, continuing to blow minds with his knowledge of feline anatomy. I wonder where he learned all of this. Some unfortunate paralegal in his firm must have an interesting internet search history.

He struts through the mostly empty room with circles of sweat beginning to stand out around the armpits of his metallic silver suit. His luxurious salt and pepper hair is carefully combed back with one lock meticulously hanging down across his forehead. Bill is a peacock in full plumage stuck inside a drab cage at the zoo. Puffed up with this much pride, Bill seems much bigger than his 5'6" frame allows. His eyes shift around the room: to the judge, making sure these punches hit home, to my wife's attorney, making sure she fully comprehends the futility of the situation she is in. Bill winks and gives me a slight knowing grin, exposing just a hint of beautifully white, perfectly capped teeth.

Surely we are winning. This is epic stuff.

My wife's sobbing gets louder. Reacting to her client's deteriorating state, her attorney opens her mouth to object to some portion of this circus, thinks better of it, and instead settles back into her chair.

I remember the sound Friskers made when I backed over him with the Porsche. It reminded me of the last squeeze of the ketchup bottle, except wetter. *SQUELCH!* Like Bill said, when I got out of the car, I saw the cat's guts had sprayed out of his ass all over my bumper, regurgitated like an overfed tick crushed by tweezers, but nothing had come out of his mouth. Friskers was still wearing his collar tightly around his neck, and it seemed to have kept any of the animal's guts from spilling out of its mouth. Liquid under pressure will always seek the path of least resistance. In Friskers' case, that was his cat ass.

I consider interrupting Bill to clear up the minor discrepancy about the ass and the mouth, but it's probably not that important. He is too deep in the flow now, up to his knees, wading through the expensive words he learned at law school and honed to a sharp point through twenty-five years of practice. Now satisfied that the scientific portion of his performance is hitting home with the judge, Bill begins explaining the legal significance of Friskers being dead before I popped him like a tube of toothpaste. I let him go on, at $450 an hour, it's best to leave it to the professionals.

I turn my attention to my wife across the table. She holds a napkin tightly in her hand, trembling as the sobs wrack her body. One small piece of translucent snot yo-yos in and out of her left nostril. She looks terrible. That's probably my fault, too.

I sit mesmerized by Mary's show as Bill drones on. This is some performance. Mary is the Best Supporting Actress Academy Award Nominee to Bill's scenery eating, leading man bombaster-y. Maybe she really did care for that cat. Even after twelve years together, ten of them married, two kids, thousands of hours spent sleeping side by side and hundreds of unfulfilling sexual encounters, I still have no read on her. Every emotion shrouded in mystery, we might as well be strangers. Roommates.

Adrenaline hits my veins like a Mack truck as the cat suddenly starts slipping out of my grasp. Distracted by Mary and the snot above her lip, I failed to notice the fur has been sloughing off his tail and Friskers has been slowly making his way down. It's too late to do anything about the nightmare taking place between my fingers. My left hand sits dead beneath the table, content to watch its twin fail spectacularly.

Bill, gesticulating wildly, is back on the hard science, explaining to the judge the technical aspects of rigor mortis in the common house cat, but everyone in the room is staring at me, realizing what was going to happen before I did. They watch enthralled as Friskers slowly slides out of my grip and thumps down loudly on the table in front of me before settling in my lap. His tail, worn down to the bone, still extends above my face. My hand is slick with the cat's bright orange hair. My lawyer is the last one to notice the slow car wreck taking place in front of me. Realizing the room is no longer wrapped around his little finger, Bill pauses mid-sentence, pivots towards me and faces the horror.

Friskers is sitting in my lap, well, most of him. On the way down, his head clipped the table and with an audible *POP!* disconnected from his brittle little body. The cat's face now turns towards me, bulging eyes still staring back, his mouth opens, and says, "This is not going well, Joel."

Oh, fuck off, Friskers.

"You should get some sleep. You've been slowly falling apart for a while now, but it's becoming obvious how strung out you are."

Nice, a dead, decapitated cat is critiquing me.

At the back of the room a man with stringy blond hair sips coffee and quietly nods. I don't know what right he has to agree with this cat. I don't know what right Friskers has to be dispensing life advice. As far as I could tell, his existence centered around his tongue and asshole. Dead cats don't have interesting opinions.

Rubbing my face with my furry right hand, I notice Bill is shooting me a look and mouthing, "Pull it together."

Even though he is now in two pieces, I must admit that little orange fuck is right. I don't sleep anymore and haven't for days. At night, I lie in bed watching *SportsCenter* repeats until the sun comes up, memorizing that day's top ten plays in nauseating detail until it's washed from my memory by the next twenty-four-hour cycle. Rinse and repeat.

I can't believe Bill convinced me to keep the cat in my freezer for the past three weeks.

I look up at the rest of the room through my fingers and can feel Friskers' hair stuck to my eyebrows. Everyone's full attention is settled on me but Bill's gaze bores the deepest hole in my skull. Interrupted, his performance castrated, he begins to shrink back from the glorious heights he had reached proselytizing in my defense, no longer the peacock. I can't wait to see his invoice.

I look around the room trying to gauge everyone's reactions to Frisker's speech, but the eyes are focused on me not the cat corpse lying in parts. Surprisingly, no one is afraid to make eye contact with me. To date, I think this has been my most public break from reality. I would assume a man talking to a dead cat in a courtroom would be threatening, but there are smiles hidden around the room. Apparently, I am more clown than serial killer.

This is just the latest form my emasculation has taken.

Also, it is probably not the best time to explain the cat had it coming.

Unable to meet Bill's murderous gaze, I turn my attention to the judge. Desperation. Silently, I beseech him to end my misery. Bringing down his gavel and calling an end to this madness would be a mercy I don't deserve but one I desperately need. A euthanizing bullet for a horse with two broken legs.

The judge peers down from his platform across the room at me. Doesn't he have a gavel? There is no gavel. He isn't wearing a robe. I don't think this is even a real courtroom. Things hadn't gotten that serious yet. After a moment, the judge stirs out of his trance and starts processing the catastrophe in front of him.

"Mr. Peterson, quite frankly, I'm not entirely sure what to make of this situation. I think I speak for everyone when I say this performance today has been extremely unsettling."

Include me in that 'everyone.'

"I will remind you and Mr. Johnson there is no need for evidence, props, or any of the production we witnessed here today. This should be a straightforward matter handled by two adults, like two adults. Do I make myself clear?"

"Yes, Your Honor," I reply. A piece of Friskers' hair falls from my eyebrow and drifts onto my tongue: the world's most disgusting orange snowflake. He makes good points. It turns out that carrying around dead cats is not a winning strategy.

"Good. Then let's end for the day. Our staff will be in touch with respective counsel to schedule another meeting next month. I do not wish to prolong the proceedings and fully expect that by the next time we meet some significant progress will have been made by each side." The judge looks down sternly one last time then disappears through a door behind his desk.

I collect Friskers' head and torso back into the large freezer lock bag I used to bring him into the courthouse. Bill reaches for my elbow and whispers something into my ear. I can't focus enough to absorb anything he's saying.

Bagged cat in hand, I beat a path to the door before everyone else. My wife's muffled sobs trail me as I navigate the labyrinth that is the recesses of the Cumberland County Courthouse. Breezing past the security I hit a heavy metal door marked "EXIT" and stumble outside.

The sunlight is blinding and fresh air refills my lungs. It's a beautiful day in southern Maine. One of the seven days a year which justifies living with the other 358 days of pain. I should be in the moment. I should stop and enjoy a day like this. A seagull circles lazily above me. Holding up the bag I look at Friskers' dumb, decapitated cat head. I wonder if the seagull is hungry for a snack. I can't keep my wife's face, red and swollen with tears, upper lip glistening with snot, from butting its way back into my consciousness. I need to find a distraction.

Across the parking lot the Porsche glints like an oasis in the desert - precision steel, glass, leather and rubber engineered into a 420 horsepower, 180-mile-per-hour sex machine. It invites me in, and I feel immediately grounded again when my hand touches the handle of the trunk. All this machine wants from me is to insert the key and twist it forward 90 degrees. The engine will spring to life in pleasure: spark plugs, rods and pistons all churning in ecstasy. When I put the car in gear and pump my right foot on the gas pedal, the drive shaft will engage and the car will glide forward. The harder I press the gas, the louder it will moan in pleasure. When I push on the brake, the car will slow and stop. When I turn the key back towards me 90 degrees, the car will turn off, and I can get out and leave it alone. The machine doesn't have any unrealistic expectations of me. It doesn't need emotional support or a partner. I can pay for it, fuck it, and that's enough, it's consistent.

I have the ability to drive this car because by most definitions, I have led a successful life. This mechanical surety is my one reward.

I fling Friskers into the trunk, then settle into the driver's seat. Turning the key, my breath catches for a second before the engine predictably roars to life reminding me there is a point to my struggle beyond crying wives, expensive lawyers and decapitated talking cats.

I pull out of the parking lot and make my way up Marginal Way towards Route 295 North. Safely ensconced in the car, I feel function return to my limbs again. Here in the womb of advanced engineering, for the first time the fog in my brain starts to burn off. No one else noticed the cat talking. Friskers wasn't smart enough alive to figure speech out; it's unlikely he evolved in death.

The Porsche moans through her muffler as I give her a little more gas: eager to please.

There are truths I have been actively fighting for the better part of my life. This whole nightmare is about more than money. It's about more than protecting the lifestyle I had worked so hard to create, the 4,500-square foot house in the posh suburb, the Porsche, or the $1.5 million sitting in cash and stocks that was tied to both of our names. I should say it's about my daughters, about fighting for something that's supposed to matter more than anything, but really it's just about right and wrong. The car and the money have always been the easiest parts for me. It's everything else I'm expected to maintain that's hard.

I pull the Porsche to a stop before the on-ramp to the highway. A homeless man is standing in the middle of the median with a sign that reads:

Out of Work
Father of two
Everyone needs a little help once in awhile
God Bless

I don't have any cash in the car, but I read an article saying more than anything homeless people want to be treated like human beings, not castaways from society. The article claimed if you don't have any money to spare, the most humane thing you can do is to make eye contact with them and acknowledge they exist in the same space as you.

I am a good person.

Craning my neck towards the driver's side window I try to maneuver my face into his view, but he stares past me towards the other cars in line.

Either the Porsche is too low to the ground or he knows not to expect handouts from middle-aged white men driving six-figure sports cars. He doesn't understand we are brothers, men beat down unfairly by the expectations heaped upon us.

I watch him in the rearview mirror as he walks down the lane. Two cars behind me, a Prius lowers the window and a hand waves a bill towards him.

The bum looks weathered: beat up Nike tennis shoes, ratty jeans and a stained NASCAR T-shirt; the perfect costume for dropping out of society. Yet even a drop-out like him eventually crawls back and begs to be let in: begging to be given a taste of society and to swim in our currency, food, booze, shelter, women, drugs, to name a few. It's amazing all the things money can buy.

How did he get to this point? Is he genetically inferior to me in some important way? Dumber? Or did a series of small but serious mistakes lead him down to the bottom? I could easily afford to give him a $100 bill every day for the rest of his life. It would literally mean nothing to me and not affect my quality of life in any way. Yet to him, that money would lift him all the way out of poverty and provide a real chance for his kids, if they're real, to succeed. I could change the course of his life. To make that decision would require courage.

I am a coward.

I want to lower my window and reach out to him and explain that I wasn't always this way. That if I had any money on me, I would give it to him. That he should expect something from men like me. That when we pass in the street he should look me in the eyes, meet *my* gaze, and acknowledge *me* as a fellow traveler, as a brother, that this ... that everything ... is about more than money or providing for a family. Life is dirty and ugly whether you beg for change in a median or fill it with smog from an excessively-priced, internally-combusting chariot; differences are only a matter of degree.

Catching my reflection in the window, I become acutely aware for the first time of how horrible I look. Four days' worth of stubble has grown in rough patches around my face. I touch my cheeks and pull down on the loose skin exposing the bloodshot whites around my pupils. I let go and the skin retreats into place reluctantly. These dark bags under my eyes are laying too many of my cards on the table for everyone to inspect. Even my expensive suit, usually impeccably tailored, hangs off me. The truth is I don't look much different than the man in the median. We're like Thanksgiving dinners: my side dishes may have been prepared by world-class chefs, but both of our turkeys are completely fucked.

He turns and starts walking back up the median towards my car. I stare straight ahead. The urgency of the moment has passed. I need to sleep. A dead cat was talking to me this afternoon.

The light turns green, and I navigate my machine away from the intersection.

CHAPTER TWO

Ga-RAGE

AS NIGHT FALLS, I can't help but watch my family cleaning the dishes after dinner through the kitchen window of the main house. For the past six months I have taken up residence in the guest house we built in anticipation that my mother-in-law would need to move in with us after Mary's father died of cancer or something. Instead, her mother met another man and has started a new life or a "second chapter" as she puts it.

Either way, I'm glad Mary allowed no penny to be spared in retrofitting the garage with a galley kitchen, den, full bath and bedroom. It provides a level of comfort I could never find at a hotel, complete with a miserable view of my family getting along happily without me.

My oldest daughter, Philomenia, eleven, blonde hair tied

back in a sharp ponytail, says something as she's drying the dishes. Mary pauses scrubbing the casserole dish and lets out a belly laugh so genuine I can sense the sound without hearing it. Hands still sudsy from the sink, she leans over and wipes the tears of laughter away from her eyes with her shirt sleeves rolled up to the elbow. She looks carefree and beautiful. My youngest, Olivia, eight, comes back into view, scrunches up her freckly nose and follows her big sister's quip with one of her own. Mary pivots and playfully flicks a handful of suds at her. I continue watching all of this in the dark. Hitting myself in the head with a cast iron pan would be less painful than watching this play.

A noise starts rustling in the freezer. I swing open the door and find Friskers' disembodied head staring back at me through the plastic bag, eyes glassy. The cat's mouth opens again. Fuck.

"Doesn't look like a family who misses their dad. Statistically girls raised without a father in the house are at a higher risk of intravenous drug use, dropping out of high school, teen runaway and pregnancy. Do you think your girls are in the same risk profile? Do they need anything other than your money?"

This cat has to go. I pull the bag out, slam the door shut and grab a shovel from the other side of the garage. Friskers hisses through the plastic.

Outside there is no moon or streetlights. Neighbors are spaced in half-acre chunks. The only thing cutting through the darkness is the yellow light emanating from the kitchen window where Mary and the girls finish up their after-dinner chores. I squint in the backyard and make out the rough shapes of topography I have become intimately familiar with: soccer net, swing set and sandbox. I swing Friskers' bag over my shoulder and shuffle towards the sandbox being careful to sidestep the square of light from the kitchen window.

With the spade, I quickly open a hole about three feet down touching into the topsoil just underneath the sand. I take special care to separate the shovels full of dirt from sand, then drop Friskers into the makeshift grave. Leaning over the hole, I check to see if the tabby has any last droplets of wisdom. Eyes now fully adjusted to the pitch-black, I can plainly see the cat staring up at me through the thin layer of plastic.

"This solves nothing," the cat warns.

Without pausing, I make quick work of the two piles, first dirt then sand. Ashes to ashes and dust to dust, etc., etc. Friskers lifeless little body belongs to the earthworms now.

Satisfied with my bit of labor, I pad back to the garage and wait for a sleep I know won't come.

CHAPTER THREE
The Desert

AS THE SUN comes up ending another sleepless night, I go about putting myself back together. I've watched enough movies to know that when you look like shit in the morning, you should splash cold water on your face and slap your cheeks dramatically with your mouth open. I try this. It does not help. The bags under my eyes are deeper and darker to the point it looks like I was knocked around by someone who really knew how to throw a punch. My skin has acquired a troubling looseness, hanging off my skull. Ordinary wrinkles have hardened into deep creases making shaving a hopeless act. If I still cared enough to do a thorough job, no doubt the razor would leave patches of stubble hidden amongst the lines in my face. Rosacea has begun weaving complicated spider webs between my cheeks and nose.

In the past, women, including Mary, have always complimented my blue eyes. One old girlfriend deep in the fog of love even described them as "piercing." Now I can see from the mirror that the blue has faded from a deep cobalt into something that belongs on the walls of a baby boy's room. The whites are bloodshot. I look like an alcoholic or drug addict. I suppose most of the people in my life assume that is what is going on. That would make sense, I guess. My life is an open book.

"Going through some tough times and hitting the bottle too hard. He'll probably kick out of it soon." I hope that is true, but the Friskers issue has me troubled. It was one thing to back over him. Stupid animal was partly to blame for lazing around behind my car, but the talking corpse was a worrisome development. Maybe I should take heart that I am still together enough to acknowledge Friskers' recent post-mortem loquaciousness is more likely a tell-tale heart than an actual phantom? I wonder. Possessed cat is an easier sell to my sanity than a ventriloquist for my subconscious.

I see through the window that the girls are waiting for the bus out front. I want to catch them before they go, so I hurriedly grab the rest of my things, slip out the door and noisily make my way down the stairs trying to attract their attention. Ollie and Philly both have their earbuds connected to their iPhones, a concession from their mother no doubt intended to make me look even worse.

"Good morning, girls," I offer, hopeful my words convey some small sliver of fatherly authority.

They both flinch at the sound of my voice but pretend not to hear. I try again this time louder. Philly raises one eye and throws me a life raft with half a nod hoping that'll be enough to move me along.

From ten feet away I can hear the pop music blaring out of their headphones. People said to expect this when we had girls, that eventually they wouldn't be so sweet. They looked sweet last night through the kitchen window.

I stand and stare at my two girls. Both pieces of me. I can see myself in Philly's eyes and in the way Ollie's jaw sets when she's nervous. I won some of the battle of nature, but appear to be losing it in nurture.

I frown and toe some loose gravel in the driveway. I feel like a desert. Scorched earth. Dried dust frying in the sun of their constant neglect. My offspring are the rain clouds of affection dispassionately passing through without regard for the ground's withering need for human contact.

None of this is right. This isn't how my life was supposed to go.

The creases on my face deepen and harden.

I want to run to them and take them in my arms. I want to hold them like I did when they were babies before life began spiraling away from me. I was a good father once. I think.

I kick a small pebble towards the garage and try to remember the good times. It's a struggle. Some pictures of us kicking a soccer ball around in the backyard float up as an offering, but they're fuzzy and I can't figure out how they ended up in my head. Even my reeling brain rejects the memories as being out of character. The thing about memories is they are entirely too subjective.

Instead of running over to the girls and shaking them, hugging them, or apologizing to them, I stand looking at them from the edge of the garage for another thirty seconds. They continue their music-fueled, stone-faced assault on my heart. Admitting defeat, I climb into the sports car watching them in the mirror as I leave the house in the rearview. I think my littlest girl, Ollie, casts me a sideways glance before they fade out of sight. Even from a great distance, I can see something pass through her eyes.

"Frances Farmer will have Her Revenge on Seattle" shuffles through on my iPod playlist. Cobain screeches out, "*I miss the comfort in being sad.*"

Fuck off, Kurt. The rest of us hung around to find out what the misery of middle age feels like and now you're dead and I can't sleep.

After two passes through the chorus, I can't take it anymore and flip off the radio. The iPod feels like the shadow of another man, one with different priorities, an enthusiasm for life unencumbered by reality. Lately, I have had very little tolerance for it.

Today is a big day. I have three cavities to fill, a root canal in the morning and an extraction in the afternoon. In half an hour, both of my hands will be in a stranger's mouth, poking holes in their teeth.

CHAPTER FOUR
$1,875,080

THE AVERAGE ADULT has twenty-eight teeth plus four wisdom teeth. In their lifetime, an adult should have at least five cavities filled ($500 each), two wisdom teeth pulled (negotiated $50 referral fee with dental surgeon), with one in ten needing full dentures ($150 referral fee). We tell our clients they need a cleaning every six months ($95) and a full set of x-rays every two years ($200). My practice has the unfortunate distinction of being located smack dab in the center of hillbilly country. It's a fight to get these people in the door at least once a year, and I don't dare raise any of my rates in an overt way.

On the plus side, white trash love soda which means our patients suffer from an unusually high number of root canals ($1,500). Our average client stays with the practice for five years generating on average $3,210 each. I pay three dental hygienists $30,000 each per year and a dental nurse $36,000. My team can support twenty-four patients per day, and with two-hundred and sixty weekdays in a calendar year, we can generate $1,840,800 per year. Upsells like crowns and teeth whitening bring in another $35,000.

One of the secret perks of practicing the great art of dentistry in Maine, besides the general lack of hygiene, is many of my customers still deal in cash, which of course I don't report and which of course adds thirty percent back to my margins. What Uncle Sam doesn't know won't hurt him.

The business has been debt-free for the past six years, and after rent ($5,000/month), salaries, benefits, a reasonable bonus for staff, my costs on drugs, toothbrushes, toilet paper and the like, plus $100,000 set aside for new equipment and upkeep, I have a slush fund of over a $1,000,000 a year to support my salary and personal expenses.

It used to be that working my cash flow statement through my mind would be enough to get me sleeping like a baby. Visions of compounded molars oozed pus and $100 bills. My little drills plunging the depths of a dead tooth and springing up dead president geysers. Instead of furry little animals jumping over fences, the little Benjamins were depositing themselves in my bank account and then kindly compounding themselves by three percent every year. Huge sums of money used to be an effective salve on my misery. Lately, it hasn't been enough—I can't pinpoint what has changed.

By the time I've put on my whites and scrubbed up, the first patient is already waiting for me in the chair. Cindy, the nurse, is finishing up the prep. We advertise a pain-free root canal; I don't think that'll be the case today.

"How's it going, Bob? You been dealin' with that tooth okay?" I ask with some trademark Maine-y downhome cheer.

"Nawt szoo good, Doc. Hafen't hawd a good night's sweep since this swept up on me. Can't rweawwy eat noffin' neeeva."

Bob is having a hard time not drooling all over himself. I recognize the bags forming under his eyes from my mirror this morning.

"Yup, yup, I bet. Nasty infection you got going on in that back molar. We'll get you all fixed up," I assure him, snapping the face mask around my ears, covering my nose and mouth. "Now, I should warn you, you're probably going to experience a fair amount of discomfort, but it's important you stay as still as possible so we can push through and get this done. Okay?"

Cindy tilts the chair back and inserts the plastic guards into the space between Bob's molars and his cheeks, propping his mouth open. *Root canal* is one of those touchy terms in the industry. The reputation of being extremely painful has been well earned, if not a little outdated. Truthfully, if I wanted to, Bob wouldn't feel anything. Truthfully, Bob doesn't even really need a root canal. He came in last week for his biannual cleaning and one of my hygienists found a common cavity in his bottom left second molar. I came in to inspect and poked around the tooth with a pick chipping away at the enamel inflaming the nerve.

Unfortunately for Bob he has insurance and I've been in a foul mood. The next forty-five minutes are going to be pretty shitty for him too. I can save over $50 in costs by not breaking open the Xylocaine and, well, more for me.

Cindy flips on the little compressor-powered system and the

drill hums lightly in the holster. I pick it up, depress the trigger, then lean into Bob's mouth. His pain is immediate, and he almost jolts out of the chair. I lean in harder pushing more of my body weight down across his torso.

"Sorry, Bob, this one is in a tricky spot. We're going to have a fair bit of drilling to get through before we're able to extract that nerve. Try to stay still," I explain, doing my best to keep him pinned down to the chair.

"MMMMHMJGHHH!" he screams, writhing violently underneath me.

"Yep, I know, but please stay as still as possible. I don't want the drill to slip and nick a healthy tooth."

I lean in harder. The crown of the molar is quickly falling away in microscopic chunks under the pulsing of my drill, testing the limits of Mr. Sucky as it struggles to keep up with the blood, spit and teeth fragments. With a clearer view now, I can see the damage I inflicted during his last visit. Exposed to the air, food and water for a week, the nerve withered and shrunk, dying. A decent-sized abscess has formed at the base of the root along the gum line. It shimmers in the fluorescent lights like a diseased pearl. That could cause some pretty expensive complications down the road.

I pull back and hand the drill to Cindy. Silently, she takes it and hands me a pick. I make quick eye contact with Bob before plunging back into his mouth. Tears stream down his face as he white knuckles the armrests. Out of a sense of curiosity more than anything, I allow my pick to puncture the abscess. Bob's body straightens out and muscles tighten as if he was being electrocuted. The pain must be intense; he doesn't even make a sound as my pick pushes deeper into the infection. All of the air exits from his lungs and he gasps like a fish out of water. This is where the root canal's reputation really pays off. He's actually paying me to torture him.

It takes about twenty more minutes, but I finally finish up with Bob. He lies straight in the chair still staring at the ceiling; his nerves overloaded from the pain. Cindy dabs at the edges of his mouth with some gauze, trying to clean up the blood before it stains his lips and scares away the other patients. Mr. Sucky fell off the pace around minute fifteen.

I snap off my plastic gloves and exhale cathartically. "Good to see you again, Bob. You should start to notice a significant reduction in the pain by tomorrow morning. If not, give us a call and we'll fit you in ASAP. From time to time we see some lingering infections at the site of the old root, so it's important to stay on top of it," I say without offering him a hint that anything he just underwent was abnormal.

Bob's eyes don't move. I pause and watch him for thirty seconds. Cindy packs more gauze into the corner of his jaw. Bob doesn't blink. He looks like a cadaver except for his chest still moving up and down.

No one has died in my chair yet. That's something.

"Well, when Cindy finishes up with you, stop by Michelle at the front desk, and we'll schedule you for a follow-up next week to make sure things are healing up all right." I force a cheeriness into my tone.

No reply. Bob remains comatose.

"Okay, well take care." And I move on to a different room. Another $1,500 in the till and another $95 in the queue.

The office is set up like what I imagine an old-time prison looked like, a perfect rectangular box: intake desk and waiting area running along the front, four three-walled hygienist stations and a surgery room run perpendicular through the middle like cells. Along the long outer wall is a narrow stocking room where all the drugs, toothbrushes and excess equipment are kept.

I enter the stockroom and lock the door behind me. My movement wakes a sensor that brings a string of overhead fluorescent lights buzzing to life making the white walls and tile floor feel even more antiseptic. My footsteps ring loudly in the tight room. There is nothing to absorb the noise: only some old metal racks I bought out of salvage and an old safe where I keep the money I don't want Mary to know about.

When I moved the practice here, I paid $35,000 to have the windows removed and an inch of steel placed between the outer brick wall and the studs holding up the drywall. This room is Fort Knox hiding my drugs from the zombies roaming around outside.

Here's a little-known fact: Dentists have all the good drugs.

Here's another one: It's really easy for some of these delicious little vials to get lost.

In high school, I messed around a little bit with some of the softies: marijuana, mushrooms, crushed up pills of various origins and potencies, and whatever else would cycle through my little town. I wasn't much different than most of my friends. On Friday, we'd find out whose parents were going to be away for the weekend and then spend Saturday night sprawled out in their basement passing around whatever skunk weed someone had been able to steal out of their older brother's room.

College was when things really started to progress more rapidly. My undergraduate work included massive amounts of research on the effects of cocaine on the brain of young white males.

During spring break of my sophomore year, I stayed in the dorms, sniffing anything I could find. People came back tanned from expensive trips to sunny places to find me sitting in the dark with the curtains drawn, arranging and rearranging my dorm furniture over and over again. With the help of an ex-girlfriend, I was able to pull out of that spiral, but the seeds had been sewn.

Part of the appeal with dental school was the unfettered access to pharmaceutical grade drugs without the pressures that come with being a surgeon or treating cancer patients. I figured I could write my own scrips, keep my head just above water, and no one would die if I fucked up.

At some point, I met Mary and cleaned up for her and then for the girls. Stopping this time wasn't that hard for me. I didn't need rehab, methadone, or anything like that. I just stopped. I had everything I was supposed to want. I was a winner. I sat around watching the girls get bigger and smarter. I kept waiting for life to deliver me the satisfaction of being a winner. I kept waiting for my just desserts. And I waited and I waited, and I got itchier and itchier. Soon enough, I started slipping back into old habits.

It was easy to maintain a small stream of morphine coming through the office—just enough to top me off and even things out until life got around to providing me with meaning. Looking back on all these years, it's easy to connect the dots as the orders of morphine got larger and more frequent.

Also, if I'm being honest with myself, it was probably a combination of physical dependency and maintaining the self-image I had built up around drugs. Has any sober person ever led an interesting life or done anything worth talking about? I've always been acutely aware of what I am. People love to poo-poo and look down their nose at addicts, but they have no problem reading their books, listening to their music, or cheering them on as they hit a baseball or tackle a running back in the backfield. Some men grow up, get married, have kids, then buy a motorcycle and a leather jacket. I inject trace amounts of morphine between my toes. We all find the meaning of things where we can.

Nowadays, the morphine has been all but impossible to come by, especially as my appetite has grown after the separation. It's forced me to resort to less conventional methods of getting high. At first, the stockroom was a veritable cornucopia of choice. Liquids and pills of every color and taste, all designed to numb, numb, numb. For years, I was an impassive expert. Now I am a connoisseur.

I walk through the room noting how empty the metal rack looks along the wall. It's hard keeping myself fed on the supplies of a small-town practice like mine. Push too hard and you're sure to attract unwanted attention. The more strung out I became, the harder it was to keep up with all the administration necessary to maintain a legal supply.

Two months ago, I recognized I was heading downhill again and took back the keys to the room from the girls who work out front. I didn't want anyone seeing how sparse it was becoming in here.

At the far end of the room is the rack holding the last of my anesthetics: a half vial of lidocaine and one dose of mepivacaine. After those, I'm down to fucking around with topical analgesics.

I'd rather avoid that.

Today is Tuesday; my next shipment comes on Thursday. Now that I've eaten through the backlog I had accumulated through the years; the weekly orders only replenish me for about three days—four if I slow down. I don't feel like slowing down. I feel like speeding up.

None of the options left are appealing. All of the "caines" I have access to aren't satisfying the itches that need scratching. What I really want are the drugs that plug directly into my brain and whisper their sweet nothings until I fall asleep. I wonder what would happen if I just drink the lidocaine. I hold up a small plastic vial to the light and shake it back and forth. With a shrug, I rip open the package tilt back the vial and drain it down my throat.

Immediately, the liquid causes my tongue to go numb then my throat. That was stupid. I had planned on leaving Cindy alone to fill the three cavities, but I still have one extraction to take care of before I leave today. This day just got more difficult.

I am not a man who has acquired many street smarts in my life. I don't have connections and am frankly afraid of what getting some would actually mean. Even in college, distractions were always too easy to find. All the things I know about drugs or drug culture I learned in movies or *Law and Order*.

The only hookup I've been brave enough to cultivate in my rich little enclave is with the Richards' kid down the street. He went to college and got into a whole bunch of freaky hippy shit. At the end of his freshman year when he came home for the summer, I bought five doses of acid. During his Thanksgiving break, seven more. Realizing he had a fish on the line, over his winter break, he brought me back a four-ounce bottle of some clear liquid. It cost me two grand. He told me it was his own formula like he's some sort of chemist or something. I may have been the victim of price gouging. Smart boy.

But what options did I have? I couldn't exactly take it to a lab and have it examined; the mystery is part of the appeal I guess. I didn't miss the two grand anyway.

The first time I took it, I swigged almost a quarter of the bottle. Rookie mistake. Since then I've limited myself to single drops from an eye dropper, which is more manageable.

Fishing the bottle out of my pocket I add a drop to my tongue. Even through the lidocaine, I sense the bitterness enveloping my nose and mouth.

Cindy looks up as I walk back into the procedure room. I can see in her eyes the Bob fiasco from this morning has her shaken. I don't like that look. Things probably went a little too far; I might be losing it more than I would like to admit.

"Everything awwlll right?" I slur. It feels like a giant dead slug is occupying the space my tongue formerly inhabited. Who drinks lidocaine?

Cindy locks eyes with me. From the red it's obvious she spent her lunch break crying.

"That wasn't good, Joel. I don't know what happened. I don't know why we didn't use an anesthetic, what we—you did to him was awful. It was medieval. He sat in the chair for another thirty minutes after you left the room. And then you just disappeared. I tried to find you, but you were just gone," she stammers through tears.

I can tell it took a lot of courage for her to speak up to me like this, but I'm not in a great state to deal with human beings right now. This conversation isn't working for me.

I look at Cindy with what I hope resembles compassion and shrug. It's the best I can do. Cindy takes a long look at me, gives up and continues prepping the station. Disappointing women seems to happen not just at home.

When her work is done, Cindy takes a deep breath, flattens her scrubs and bravely steps out into the waiting room to welcome the next patient. Even high, I recognize getting through today has just about drained her. She's almost to the finish line.

The clear liquid is starting to kick in harder. I can feel the drift starting.

Cindy leads the second patient into the room and seats her on the chair. I know her name is Joan Cumberland. I know she is a forty-five-year-old receptionist, mother of three, with insurance. I know she has auburn hair but is otherwise unremarkable. I know all of this because Joan has been a patient for five years. However, looking at Joan under the influence of hallucinogens cooked up in some frat boy's basement is far different than looking at Joan under the sober light of morning. I keep my cool as a worm wiggles out of her hair and into her ear.

Joan looks up at me and smiles as Cindy fusses with the drool guard that goes around her neck. She waits for me to say something, but all I can do is stare. Unlike Bob, Joan's issues are entirely genuine—the result of a rather nasty three-a-day Mountain Dew habit.

File, take a sip of soda.

Pick up the phone; take a sip of soda.

Forward an email; take a sip of soda.

Ignore her boss' comment about what she could do to look better in that dress; take a sip of soda.

And on and on, forever and ever, amen.

Everyone has a crutch, but she might as well be drinking battery acid. Forty-five-years-old and her teeth feel like they are made of chalk. I can't imagine what her insides look like. I could start spending the money now that she's going to have to pay me for dentures in five years. Joan is a rather plain woman leading what I imagine is a rather plain life.

My throat is now completely numb. Touching it is the only way I can confirm my head is still attached to something.

"Good afternoon, Doctor," she says perfunctorily after Cindy gets her settled. I nod in response and turn my back to hide my wild grin as I set out the tools.

I love it when they call me doctor. Some of the men that come through this place see the Porsche in the parking lot and make a sport of taking me down a peg. I don't waste the good drugs on assholes. This may be Joan's lucky day.

Reclining back in the chair with her mouth spread open in a frozen grin by the plastic spacer, Joan stares at the ceiling and avoids eye contact. I lean in and look at the horror that is her mouth. The second lower bicuspid is gray and clearly dead, the first of many soldiers sure to be downed under the guns of General Dew. I finger it absentmindedly, Joan flinches. I should tie this tooth to a door and slam it shut, old school. The gums around it look like overcooked steak. I would be surprised if it even bleeds.

I pull back from her mouth and consider a lecture on the bottled acid that she drinks every day, but honestly at this point, I don't give a fuck. At the moment my tongue is not exactly in pristine working order. Cindy clears her throat. Time to get down to it.

As Cindy goes back to prepping Joan, I head back into the bare stockroom. The last vial of mepivacaine sits glistening on the empty shelving. I stop and stare at it paralyzed by indecision. I don't have the patience to deal with Cindy again so I grab the painkiller and a syringe, then lock the door behind me.

Cindy looks up as I enter the room. I register the relief in her eyes when she sees the drug in my hand. What a hero I am.

"Alright, Joan, we're going to get started here. You'll feel a little pinch as I administer the numbing agent and then nothing. This dosage should last us through the extraction, but let me know if it starts wearing off." I concentrate hard to control my dead slug tongue. She doesn't need to know if it does wear off, there's absolutely nothing I can do to get more.

Joan briefly scans my eyes and gives a subtle shrug. I take it to indicate she understands. Her eyes look grey like her tooth and sad. She is resigned to it so I go about my business administering the mepivacaine. Within two minutes, her mouth is completely numb.

Behind her head I lift the pliers off the tray. I learned through experience, when dealing with some of the more medieval tools of my trade, it is always better to not let the patients get a good look at what I am going to use inside their mouths.

With a firm grip on the dead tooth, I rock it back and forth. The little booger holds on tight in there. I give it a twist as it rocks, and the roots start breaking free from the gums, crunching as the enamel pulls away from the flesh. Finally, it bends forward at a ninety-degree angle and I clear it from the final pieces of dead meat.

Through all of this, even as I'm twisting a piece of her skull out of her mouth, Joan remains firmly focused on the ceiling. She never flinches. For Cindy, this seems to be a welcome relief from the drama of the morning's root canal; the sense of relief in the room is palpable even to me.

But something in Joan's demeanor is troubling. Usually even during extractions covered by a drug all the crunching and pulling draws a reaction from the patient. Joan just stares straight ahead the whole time, seemingly as dead inside as her rotten tooth. I study her blank expression as Cindy goes about cleaning up her mouth and the trace amounts of blood. Joan looks like I feel, and I don't appreciate the mirror. What the fuck does she have to be so sad about?

"Joan, is something boffering yew? Is the medicine wearing off?" I slur through my lazy tongue.

She shifts uncomfortably in the seat and finally breaks the death stare she had with the ceiling. "No, I can't feel anyfing yet," she lisps.

I hardly hear her answer. The vial from the Richards' kid is starting to really kick in. I think I might need to throw up. I'm reaching that familiar point where it is tough to be sure of anything.

"Right, well, might be wise to avoid eating anyfing for the next few hours. In your state, it would be easy to bite your tongue or cheek. I've seen people do some real damage to demselves thaa way," I offer to Joan as sweat starts popping up on my brow.

Her blank stare continues.

"Did Michelle talk to yew when you came in? We're offering in-house financing now if yew want us to put a falsie in thaa gap we made today. Twenty percent down, ten percent interest, sewenty-two months?" I don't know why I insist on extending our little interaction. My sweat glands are going full steam now, quickly soaking the collar of my white scrubs.

Joan continues sitting in the chair, staring coolly at the ceiling. I wait a beat. No response. My heart races and my vision doubles then bounces back into focus. The worm makes its way back out of her ear and perches above her eyebrow. It considers me with tiny, beady, black eyes. I take a glance at Cindy. She is still making herself busy tidying up the station.

I can't see the worm's mouth move but my head fills with its voice. "There is a fine line between nostalgia and depression."

Fine, yes, Worm, I agree.

"Unrealistic expectations fostered in large part by mainstream beer advertising contributes to the culture of rape found across college fraternities."

A little myopic maybe, but okay, I can buy that.

"Social media will first save humanity and then destroy it."

It's natural to be hesitant about things you can never understand.

"Your rabid materialism and navel-gazing self-obsession has ruined your relationship with your daughters and severely compromised their chances of ever being able to truly trust a man or relate to another human being."

Well, Worm. Now we're getting somewhere, aren't we? You sound just like a cat I once knew.

Satisfied with the messages delivered, the Worm blinks its microscopic eyes twice and retreats into Joan's ear.

I realize two things simultaneously: one, my throat has become alarmingly numb, making swallowing a most difficult task, causing the front of my white scrubs to become drenched in spit. Without an undershirt, the scrubs are now transparent revealing my chest hair and nipples. Two, amidst all the drool, my eyes have been fixed on Joan for an indeterminate yet likely inappropriately long period of time.

Life snaps back into focus for a second. Both Joan and Cindy are staring at me. Cindy's bottom lip appears to be trembling. I catch a reflection of myself in the hand mirror hanging over Joan, eyes at a thousand-yard stare, drooling profusely, sweating with nipples standing alertly through my shirt. There is no avoiding the truth: I appear monstrous.

My mouth closes quickly, barely avoiding my slug tongue as it retreats toward my throat. I do my best to wipe the remaining spit off my chin. This situation is not salvageable. No combination of words in the English language have been invented which could explain this away. I take advantage of the momentary sobriety and beat a hasty retreat out of the room.

Back in the safety of the storage room, I turn off the lights and sprawl out across the floor. The cool concrete is sobering. I move so little that the motion sensor lights turn off entombing me in blackness. Through the crack at the bottom of the door, I watch shadows dance back and forth and listen to the idle chit-chat between the girls and the day's remaining customers. Eventually, they pack up and head home back to their lives. I stay still in the blackness, staring at an unseen ceiling, afraid to move.

CHAPTER FIVE
A Liar and a Thief

THE CONCRETE FLOOR is merciless on my back. The shop has shut down for what must be hours and the girls have locked down the building. Even with no other options, my brain refused to give and let me sleep. Instead, I was subjected to the torture of life-size projections of my failures floating on the ceiling above. Mostly it was Ollie's face in the rearview mirror as I drove away. Each time the loop picked up a little bit farther down the road from her, and each time I registered her disappointment a little more clearly. Eventually, I cycled off whatever that Richards' kid gave me and that nightmare was replaced by a never-ending blackness.

Stopping by the bathroom, I confront the mirror to inspect the damage. Hmmm, greasy hair, face sunken, eyes bloodshot. Deep, darkly-creased cheeks tightly lined with a stubbly beard. My watch shows 2:30 in the morning. Almost eleven hours lost to the ether—a horribly sobering ether.

I open the door to the stockroom and step into the office. It's empty. The girls locked up for the night, but they didn't set the alarm. They must have known I was still in the room. I grab my keys from the ring, punch in the code and make my way out into the parking lot.

Free from the stale air of the stockroom, I breathe in deeply, passing the coolness of the night through my lungs. The world around me is still, and the Ferris wheel inside my head has slowed. Streetlights hum above the pavement, illuminating my parking lot in bright yellow cones. Nothing looks monstrous. The path to my car appears free of opinionated invertebrates.

The Porsche calls back to me as I trigger the remote, then roars to life as I settle in the front seat and turn the key. With my hands on the wheel, I can feel the machine vibrating like a wild animal on the hunt. Sinews and muscles coursing beneath a rugged skin as it imagines the kill. I rev the engine twice for good measure, then put the car in gear and pull out into the night.

Crisp air flows across my face as I hit forty-five with the windows down. In the early morning I can feel the dew forming on my skin. The clarity provided by sobriety makes my problems seem manageable again. Downshifting, the Porsche roars in agreement, eating up the pavement.

I think I'll enjoy this ride and take the empty backroads home. At home, I'll park the car in the garage and try to catch two hours of sleep in my little apartment. I'll set the alarm for 6:15, wake up without hitting the snooze, then shower, shave and put on a fresh white t-shirt. I'll head over to the main house and make pancakes for the girls before they head off to school: strawberries for Philly, blueberries for Ollie. With the girls out of the house, I'll give Mary a back rub, apologize and explain that I am going to change.

No more drugs.

No more lying.

No more dead pets.

No more obsessing about money.

No more fucked-up priorities.

I'll beg for her forgiveness. I'll get down on my knee like when I proposed to her. I'll cry. We'll cry. She'll forgive me. We'll make love. Our girls will grow up happy and fulfilled. I'll retire when they graduate from college. Mary and I will travel the world. I'll dote on my grandchildren. I'll die before Mary as her cherished husband. She'll be devastated and then be buried beside me.

I'll go home, sleep, then do all these things. A full cold-turkey reset on my life.

I push my foot into the gas pedal accelerating the machine to eight-five. The scenery blurs unrecognizable as the Porsche continues ratcheting up across the slick black top. The car's back end shudders then skates across the pavement. With both hands, I torque the wheel to the left, trying to keep it in contact with the tar. For a brief, glorious second it seems to grab the road and I have hope, but the contact is lost as quickly as it was found. The car careens across the yellow lines into the other lane. I was foolish to think I could control a wild animal.

I will never know for sure, but I think I hear *Pennyroyal Tea* by Nirvana pass through the radio as the car speeds airborne over the embankment and towards the tree line. Time stops as gravity loses its hold on me. I watch as my wallet and phone hit the ceiling.

Astonished, I register the detail on Abe Lincoln's beard as pennies in my cup holder spin in flight.

Joan appears in the passenger's seat with blood slowly trickling out of her mouth and dead eyes staring through the windshield—an apathetic witness to the oncoming carnage. I know what is happening even though I don't. She flickers like a scratched VHS twice and then I am alone again.

The car's flight reaches its apex, and I feel us start to plummet back towards Earth. Life begins to make sense. I am a helpless observer of my own journey; powerless to stop the disasters I see coming and uninterested in stopping the ones I don't. The car's front end contacts the earth. Somewhere I imagine Cobain watching with amusement. The front bumper hits a stump and the car starts to flip.

I also am a liar and a thief.

I also am so tired I can't sleep.

But then I do.

CHAPTER SIX
Professional Courtesy

LIKE A FERN dropping a spore, a tiny, naked Bill Johnson drops off my lawyer's finger and runs across the room. I sit paralyzed, watching as Little Bill scales my pant leg, up the buttons on my shirt and grabs hold of my chin. I can hear his microscopic little lungs panting from exertion. Tiny droplets of sweat stream down his chubby torso and run onto my collar. With a soft grunt, Little Bill pulls himself aside my nose and pops into the hole Big Bill has bored into my forehead. My eyes turn inward as I watch Little Bill, apparently furious, jumping around on my brain, digging at it like a dog with a bone to hide at the beach. He rips into the soft grey matter with his teeth, releasing springs of spinal fluid and blood, rubbing the mess all over his fat cherubic body. My face twitches involuntarily as he takes little pieces of think-y flesh and throws them in the air like confetti. Friskers watches the commotion from the corner near my left ear and purrs quietly as he cleans himself.

Outside Big Bill is explaining his latest invoice. "Listen, Joel, I know you've had a rough time of it lately, and I know we've spent quite a bit more than we estimated at the outset, but this case has really had some hair on it." Bill winces slightly at his choice of words.

I mumble something incoherent as Little Bill pulls on a particularly sensitive area. I think it sounds like "GROUPER SLUT," but truthfully, I am in no position to judge.

Big Bill doesn't seem to mind. He rolls on, "So if you'll just sign this, we'll get another fifty-grand transferred into my IOLTA account. That should be enough to let me continue to work on your behalf for the next three months or so."

To my surprise a pen is hastily jammed into my hand and placed on top of a sheet of paper with a lot of numbers and letters, none of which seem to be in any kind of distinguishable order. Friskers scratches at me, prances in a circle, then nests down. The sensation causes me to flinch and my hand scribbles some random marks on the paper.

Bill looks at the sheet and appears satisfied with my penmanship. "Great, thanks Joel. Listen, don't worry a bit, we're going to get this all fixed up ASAP. While you were ... umm, out, I got the judge to push back our next meeting for a month," he announces excitedly.

Out? How long have I been out? I try to ask Bill what he means by *out* but it ends up sounding like "MUFFIN CUNT TURBO SPANK!"

Friskers meows lazily.

Unfazed, Bill continues, "Yeah, you still seem a little fucked up. The good news is the doctors told me structurally you're okay. Once you regain some motor control, there is no reason you shouldn't be able to walk and lead a normal life again."

Life rushes in around Bill and I notice my surroundings. Yes, this is a hospital. I am lying in a mechanical bed wearing nothing but a hospital gown with wires connecting me to a number of exotic beeping apparatuses. The gown feels itchy and cheap.

Something in my look must have alerted Bill and he grabs the paper from underneath my hand, then heads towards the door while I struggle to regain full lucidity. I can't let him go yet; I have a very important question he needs to answer.

My brain thrashes, desperate to regain its footing. I remember now. The little vial of magical liquid. Lying on my back in the storeroom. Resolving to fix my pathetic life. Driving home. Crashing the car. But it seems like I am alive and I am in the hospital and things were going to change.

"DEE THE GWEELS VEESSIT ME?" It comes out like a scream, my neck tendons pushing against my skin.

"Joel, relax. Don't overdo it. You've been through so much."

I sit up and strain to take control of my synapses back from Little Bill and Friskers. "DEE THE GWERLS VEESIT ME?" Better.

Bill stares at me still confused.

I inhale deeply and concentrate. My brain begins rippling with electromagnetic energy. Little Bill sees the writing on the wall and tries to run but a massive energy storm has begun making its way across my grey desert, zapping him into a pile of dust. Friskers jumps up and grabs hold of the top of my skull with all four paws like he used to do to the curtains. He too is quickly rendered into nothing by the urgent force of my question.

Very slowly all the energy from my cerebral cortex is diverted from every vital function and funneled to my lips. My heart skips a beat as I concentrate on forming the words that will decide my fate. I feel like Uma Thurman trying to wiggle her toes. "DID. THE. GIRLS. VISIT. ME?" Breathing heavily from the exertion, I stare down my lawyer, summoning all my psychic powers.

Bill looks at me with a mixture of pity and disgust and pauses before answering. I don't want to hear the answer anymore.

His tone softens. "Joel, she's been through a lot. Look, I'm sure the kids wanted to, but in your condition and with all the drugs they found," Bill pauses. It's just ... I don't know ... try and see it from her perspective. I think she's worn out. Also, about the drugs, they are going to complicate things."

Fuck.

"Glad you're doing better. We'll talk soon," he ends on a chipper note, turns and is gone.

A nurse passes Bill just outside and enters the room. She is dressed neatly in clean scrubs with her hair pulled back tightly in a ponytail. She looks pleasant and professional. We make eye contact as she goes about her business in my room. She seems surprised to see a spark of intelligence behind my eyes. The conversation with Bill was like cold water on my senses, and suddenly I am full of questions.

"What happened?" my tongue feels thick and stupid.

The nurse comes over to the foot of my bed and answers, "You were in an accident and flipped your car into a thicket of trees out in central Cumberland. Some kids coming back from a party found you. The fire department brought out the Jaws of Life and pried you out of the car. You are pretty lucky to even be alive. I guess those folks at Porsche sure know how to make a car."

They sure do. "How long have I been here?" My throat burns from all this talking. She notices and pours me a glass of water from the sink. I gulp it greedily while she answers.

"Five days. You were in a medically induced coma for the first two and then we've been trying to wake you up for the last three. You just didn't seem to respond to coming off the meds. I guess your body needed the extra rest. It's nice to see you becoming more coherent. The doctors were all very concerned you might have some significant brain damage. We'll have to run more tests, but this is great progress. We should have your lawyer in more often." She laughs quickly at her little joke.

Don't threaten me, woman.

For the first time, I become aware of my body. It hurts. A lot. The nurse watches as I gingerly pull back the covers and take inventory. Two feet, five toes each, two arms, one hand each with five full fingers. There are casts on my left wrist and ankle, but with some effort, I can still wiggle the toes and fingers on that side. In fact, all the extremities respond to my mental impulses albeit with varying levels of dexterity. Everything is connected. Speaking of which, I grab between my legs and am relieved to find that where I left it.

She notices my inspection and adds helpfully, "The car was lying on the driver's side with your arm and leg crushed by the door. They were both clean breaks, which we were able to set. When the casts come off, you'll be as good as new."

I wonder what her definitions of "new" or "good" are.

I request a mirror and she brings one over to the bed. The stubble has grown into a decent beard which has in turn become a receptacle for bed lint, snot, spit and a million other little horrors. But my eyes are clear and my skin has reclaimed a measure of healthy elasticity I had lost during the past two months.

"Umm, if you're feeling up to it, I can tell the doctor you're awake. I know there are some things he wants to discuss with you," she says more tentative now.

I am full of joy. "Actually, I'm not feeling up to it quite yet, what with just waking up from a week-long coma and all. Howsabout we get some food in me and let me process my newfound consciousness for at least a couple of hours?" I take another long draw from the glass of water.

"Sure thing," she responds with fake cheer. "I'll grab you a menu and let the doctor know you're awake and recovering nicely."

She bounces out of the room and it's just me again with all my thoughts. I eye the phone sitting on the table. I should call Mary. That is a terrible idea. A deliciously terrible idea. I shudder unconsciously. That phone is nothing but trouble.

The nurse steps back into the room with a menu, placing it on the edge of the bed. "Just dial nine when you're ready, and they'll send it up to the room."

I eye the list greedily. My Rip Van Winkle routine has rebooted my appetite. I'm fully awake now and apparently hungry for lukewarm, stale grilled cheese and gluey clam chowder. I grab the phone and place the order to some disembodied voice on the other end.

Before I know it, an orderly arrives with a plastic cafeteria tray containing a plate with a nuclear orange grilled cheese and a bowl of sad looking gloop. He sets it gingerly across my lap then leaves. Watching me eat this garbage would be too much for him to bear.

Even the most rudimentary risk analysis conducted after a five-day coma tells me to try the sandwich first. Without trepidation, I pull it apart with my hands and shovel the pieces down my throat.

I can feel the chowder looking at me. I dip a spoon in the bowl and pause as the grey gloop with clams nears my lips. My stomach sends a warning rumble, "No mas, señior, no mas." I ignore its pleadings and shovel the spoonful down my gullet. It hits the bottom and swishes around. I add a second, then a third and a fourth until the bowl is empty. My stomach considers the predicament I have placed it in and decides evacuation is the only option. My first meal in a week is sent violently back up my esophagus and out my nose and mouth. It tastes the same in both directions.

The nurse comes back in from the hallway. She opens the door with a doctor trailing behind her. A partially digested hunk of potato falls out of my nostril onto my lap. They pause at the threshold. I can hear the nurse sigh from ten feet away. They both enter the room, and her professionalism wins out as she sets about getting a clean set of sheets and hospital gown from the closet.

"Mr. Peterson, good to see you awake!" the doctor says with all the enthusiasm of a car salesman. He steps towards the bed and I take a hard look at him. He's in his late 50s or early 60s, thinning gray hair combed back over his head and behind his ears, unremarkable in most respects except for his nose. It protrudes from his face like a beak and is crisscrossed with red and blue blood vessels resembling a map. This is a man who likes his drink. I squint my eyes and lean closer to see if I can make out any words. Perhaps a colony of tiny people has been stranded in his nostrils and are trying desperately to get their SOS message out. I concentrate on one particularly bulbous vein which I swear is pulsing.

"Uhh, my name is Dr. Jeffery. I am the physician who has been attending to you during your stay," less cheery now; he seems shaken by how intently I am studying his face. I wonder if Jeffery is a first or last name. He seems like the sort who would want to appear friendly and approachable but is too vain to drop the Dr.

"Got it, Doc. How am I doing?" Somewhere in the background I register the nurse changing the sheets on the bed.

"Well, your vitals appear normal and your injuries will heal. You are a very lucky man, Mr. Peterson."

So I've been told. "Actually, it's Dr. Peterson. I am a DMD."

"OK, *Dr. Peterson,* there is another matter we have to discuss. One that is quite serious I'm afraid." He frowns and looks down at the papers in his hands.

"Yeah? Uh-huh, okay." Unable to discern any words, I lean in a bit closer towards his snout to see if I can spot a signal fire that any survivors may have lit.

"Well, uh, due to the nature of the accident, the police required us to run a toxicology screen on your urine, and well, uh, I thought it was important to inform you of that. Now that you are awake we are required to report your condition back to them. I believe they will be coming to discuss the results with you."

No smoke signal. Anyone who survived must be long dead by now. "Doctor Jeffery, did I mention to you that I am a DMD?" I ask.

"Uh, yes, you did." He smiles tentatively.

"Right. Well, I would sincerely appreciate a little professional courtesy in this matter." I shift away from his nightmare nose and make eye contact for the first time.

The nurse is still busying herself with sheets, pretending not to pay attention to the conversation. She's able to change the bed around me like a magician, subtly rolling me right, then left and *voilà*, new sheets.

"I happen to be going through a rather complicated custody matter with my two daughters and this is a ... umm, sensitive time." I level my best serious face at him, seeing if I can crack him through the force of my will. My sleepy brain struggles to keep up with the demands I am suddenly placing on it.

Jeffery and I stare at each other for what seems like ten seconds, long enough for the nurse to come over to me with a washcloth and dab at the puked-up chowder on my face. I had forgotten that was there. This is not going well.

Jeffery breaks the silence. "I'm sorry, Mr. Peterson, I'm afraid I can't do that. In fact, I'm not entirely sure I haven't already placed myself in a world of trouble just by letting you know we ran the screens, but, uh, I thought it was the right thing to do. You know, professional courtesy and all." A little smile passes by the corners of his mouth.

The nurse steps in again and pulls the gown over my arms and head. In nothing but my skivvies with fragments of potato and clam still clinging to my week-old beard, I refuse to break eye contact with Jeffery.

I am the untamable animal of revenge.

I am a dangerous man with dangerous skills.

I have an indomitable will.

I can control my own destiny.

The nurse asks me to raise my arms over my head then slips a clean gown down my body as Jeffery turns to leave.

I am a jellyfish floating along at the pleasure of the tide.

I am a released balloon drifting off to nowhere.

I am going to test positive for whatever I bought from that Richards' kid.

I am in the shit.

Whether from the food or the excitement, I am incredibly tired. The nurse follows Jeffrey out of the room as I slouch back into the bed defeated. A man without a family, without a country, left to drift. With nothing to do, my brain throws in the towel and I fall back asleep.

CHAPTER SEVEN
Black, Again

MY FOOT PUNCHES down on the gas, sticking the pedal to the floor. The Porsche's engine revs faster, pushing the machine cleanly along a winding road. The top is down and the cool night air tousles my hair like an affectionate, approving father. I bring it in through my nose and feel its crispness fill me up. On a straightaway now, I shift and smoothly bring the machine up to ninety.

The headlights don't penetrate the dense forest surrounding the street. Trees stand back only a few feet from the pavement. There is no room for a mistake at this speed. Even a small hiccup will send me careening into death. This takes all my skill, but still I push the engine harder, faster. The car needs me. Without this connection through my hands and feet to my brain, it is an irrelevant hunk of metal and glass. Without me, there is no one to guide it through the world. No one to push it to be all it can be. Not in some bullshit Army "Rah! Rah!" kind of way; in a way you can only know when maxing out a finely-tuned German automobile through an impenetrably dark Maine back country road with death watching curiously only a few feet away. Every second pushes me farther and farther from the hospital, from the police and from the family that left me to rot. The machine does not feel pain or abandonment, and now, neither do I. I am cleansed from caring.

Have the divorce.

Have the money.

Have the girls.

I am leaving it all behind.

I look to the passenger's seat on my right and a man is riding with me. He is gaunt with greasy, dirty blond hair circling a boyish face. Fresh stubble covers a perfectly cleft chin. Sitting in the passenger's seat without a seatbelt, his knees are pulled up to his chin; he's wearing dirty jeans full of holes and a flannel shirt. He is a stereotype, a cliché and I know immediately what this means.

"I tried hard to have a father but instead I had a dad," his voice is crusty and guttural.

I also know these words already. "I don't want to have this conversation, Kurt," I say through clenched teeth. "Can't you see? I want to be free on the open road and not lying in a hospital bed, waiting for a couple of dumb Frick and Frack cops to come ask me a bunch of questions."

It seems so obvious.

He stares straight ahead into the black beyond the headlights with knees pulled up to his mouth rubbing the skin on his kneecap across his lips back and forth. This is a man unimpressed by what I want.

"Besides, you are the very last person to critique how I raise my kids. I was rejected. You gave it up willingly. It is our job to break cycles that were started for us and not flail blindly through adulthood."

I wish he would go away.

He turns and looks at me with cold blue eyes. He is beautiful and young. There is a barely audible pop as his lips lose their suction on his skin. He says, "Your legendary divorce is such a bore," and returns to staring into the night and sucking on his knee through a hole in his jeans.

I don't have the stomach for this anymore. I let go of the wheel and slam my foot all the way to the floor. We careen off the road and for the second time, I feel the sensation of weightlessness as the car hits the embankment and flips towards the tree line.

I turn to the passenger, but he is gone and I am alone. I watch dispassionately as the car flips towards an oak.

How tiresome.

Then there is black again.

CHAPTER EIGHT
Frick and Frack

THERE IS A BEAM OF LIGHT streaming in through the blinds directly onto my face. Maybe I'm in heaven or something. I rub the sleep from the corners of my eyes, opening them a little wider to take stock of my eternal reward.

Fuck, it's only the sun. Squinting, I fumble around until I find the remote control and lever the bed up into a sitting position. Two official-looking men stand in the doorway with the nurse in front of them.

"Oh good, you're awake," she says with familiar false cheer. "You have some visitors."

Officer Frick and Detective Frack I presume. The pleasure will be all mine I'm sure. My head is throbbing. I rub my temples trying to clear out some of the madness inside. Something tells me I am going to need my wits about me. The nurse steps back and the flatfoots move into the room.

Detective Frack steps to the foot of the bed and clears his throat. He's wearing an ill-fitting blue suit that looks like it came off the distressed rack at a warehouse fire-sale. Blond hair cropped high and tight, skin smooth and new: he can't be much older than twenty-five and clearly not the grizzled vet of the force. Visiting me in the hospital is apparently not the sort of task that draws the "A Team."

"Mr. Peterson." His voice cracks and he loudly clears his throat—embarrassed. "Mr. Peterson, I am Detective Smiley."

I raise my eyebrows at the name, causing him to blush. What a curse.

Trying valiantly to keep his composure and some semblance of authority, he nods seriously towards his partner. "And this is Officer Jorgensen."

I yawn and stretch dramatically. "Okay. What can I do for you two?" Anything these cheese puffs expect to get from me they're going to have to pay for.

Sensing his authority is teetering on a ledge, Smiley balloons out his chest and puts on his best police academy tone. "Glad to see you made it through the accident all right. Officer Jorgensen was the first to the scene."

Jorgensen nods. Portly and dressed in patrol blues with his lips pursed tightly together, he looks fifteen years older than Smiley and about seventy pounds heavier. A small bead of sweat is on his brow. Based on his weight and ashy complexion, my guess is perspiration is a constant part of his day. I wonder how he likes having Smiley as a boss.

Smiley continues, "You were lucky to be driving that car. A

lesser automobile would probably have been the death of you."

Lucky, yes, also extremely rich but never mind all that.

Smiley pauses for a beat in case I have something to interject like what a lucky boy I am. Instead I make it obvious that I have nothing but silence and fierce eye contact to contribute at this time. My instincts scream Smiley is a weak link; maybe I can shake him with this indomitable will of mine.

Jorgensen inches closer behind his boss perhaps sensing paternally that I am a caged lion and Smiley may need protection. Or perhaps wanting a better view in the event there is a blood-letting of his younger, more successful colleague. Like a predator ready to pounce, lying in the weeds watching the antelope eat, I can feel my animal instincts sharpening. In this heightened state with my senses operating at a superhuman level, I smell the sweat seeping from Jorgensen's armpits.

Smiley keeps going, oblivious to the threat staring him in the face. "However, due to the circumstances of the accident, we ran some additional tests while you were recovering and your blood test came back positive for phencyclidine."

I look at him quizzically gnashing my teeth. "What is phencyclidine?" I ask.

Jorgensen clears his chubby throat, trying to draw my attention. I set my stare on the Fatty. Be warned, Tubby, best let sleeping dogs lie. Walk away now while you still can. Unfazed, he picks up where his boss left off. "The street name is PCP or angel dust."

Holy shit! PCP? That Richards' kid was feeding me PCP! I was taking PCP, angel dust. I am both moderately impressed with myself and full of dread. That's probably not the best decision I could have made.

Smiley senses the tide changing and continues on with more confidence, "As you know, Mr. Peterson, this is a very serious situation. Understand, you are not under arrest right now, but when you have sufficiently recovered, we will need to bring you into the station." He says this with full confidence; clearly this was the ax he had been waiting to drop. "We understand that in addition to the accident you are going through some personal issues with your wife. You should be aware we have been in contact with your lawyer, Johnson. Any charges filed will influence your divorce and custody rights."

Somewhere in my brain the ghost of Little Bill stirs. That ass. My custody rights?

Frick and Frack, Tubby and Crewcut, Jorgensen and Smiley have won. There is a difference between a wounded animal and a caged dog starved, beaten with a stick and used as an ashtray. I look up and Smiley has his chest puffed out, lungs now full of authority. It's obvious I have lost, as if the outcome was ever really in doubt.

Dumb, fat Jorgensen looks sorry for me. Pity from him is even worse than Smiley's pride.

I lie back on the bed and they see themselves out. The casts on my ankle and wrist itch. I have to pee. I have to shit. I need help. How much of that PCP do I have left?

CHAPTER NINE
All Alone

THIS JUDGE IS NOT A FAN OF MINE. The doctor said I could take the casts off, that the breaks in my wrist and ankle had healed. I chose to leave them on. This is a battle of optics. Neglectful, drug-abusing father against beautiful doting mother doing her best to raise two daughters on her own. Public relations professionals would call this a cluster-fuck or something. These casts should help even the odds. At least this time I left Friskers at home.

Oh shit, Friskers. With everything else going on, I'd forgotten where I left him.

Mary's lawyer stands up. "Your Honor, I'm not sure how much more evidence we need to introduce into the record that Mr. Peterson is not a fit parent. In the past month, he has destroyed his car, been charged with driving under the influence, possession of a schedule II narcotic, and two weeks ago, Little Ollie found the remains of the family cat buried in her sandbox. As you may remember, the cat was being kept by Mr. Peterson apparently as proof that he was not responsible for its death."

I can't stomach that woman referring to my daughter as "Little Ollie" like she knows her.

We have graduated to a real courtroom. The door opens in the back; I turn around and watch a visitor slip in and take a seat in the last row. Nobody else seems to notice. I guess it's not unusual for dead cultural icons to observe boring white people argue about boring white people issues. I guess what qualifies as reality T.V. is relative.

"We ask that the court terminate Mr. Peterson's visitation rights and institute a temporary restraining order for both the children and Mrs. Peterson effective immediately. With Mr. Peterson now cleared to return home from the hospital, we feel it is in the best interest of Olivia and Philomenia that Mr. Peterson be barred from returning to living in the garage on my client's property or from having any contact with the children."

Yeah, okay, but look at my arm and ankle. Have some pity on a wounded man. I look at Bill. He shrugs. I turn and look at Kurt sitting in the back. He shrugs too. I guess everyone agrees she has some pretty good points. I can't believe I forgot about burying Friskers in the girls' sandbox. I'm not sure what I could have done about it, but I probably shouldn't have completely forgotten.

The lawyer continues, "Furthermore, Your Honor, due to the unstable nature of Mr. Peterson and the strict control he has historically maintained over the family's assets, we ask all of his accounts be frozen and two-hundred thousand dollar be placed into an account only Mrs. Peterson can access. As she is currently unemployed, this will allow her to continue to support the children in the manner to which they have become accustomed as well as fund her continuing legal representation. If Mr. Peterson still wishes to contest this matter, we are prepared to enter sworn statements from both girls into evidence."

Well then. I steal a quick glance at Kurt, sitting cross-legged, his wispy frame enveloped completely by the long bench, scribbling in a notebook, apparently bored or inspired. It seems to be a fine line. He's dyed the tips of his hair red since the last time I saw him. He doesn't look up at me.

Bill sits silently next to me with his chin in his left hand, elbow propped on the table, also scribbling on a yellow legal pad. The bombast of his previous defenses has vanished. Apparently, I have broken even his spirit. I look at the paper to see what I am paying for. I don't expect much and for that reason only I am not disappointed by the intricate maze Bill has started in the upper left corner and painstakingly wound across and down the page. It's actually fairly impressive.

Despite all my rage, I am still just a rat in his maze. I cut off that thought before it takes root. My head can't deal with any more clutter. Maybe I should take some comfort in understanding I am quickly unraveling. True madness would be to think this is all normal, right? That everything is okay? Does a drowning man always realize he is drowning? Feeling that black water seep down his throat, filling his lungs. Knowing it means death is much different than being able to do anything to stop it. Knowledge is not all it's cracked up to be.

"Mr. Peterson?" the judge demands, glaring down from his perch.

"What?"

"Do you want to contest?" The judge had spent most of the proceeding turned sideways, looking at a computer screen, clearly in control but not making eye contact when anyone spoke. Now he is staring down his nose from up high, wearing that ridiculous robe, and challenging me with eye contact. He's trying to get into a crazy eyes contest with a crazy person. There's a reason you don't stare at the man lying on the street in a pool of his own vomit begging for cat food.

I focus all my menace into my pupils crystalizing the black sludge oozing inside of me into icicles ready to fly forth from my eyes piercing his arrogant, judgmental resolve.

The judge meets my stare unflinching. He must think he has seen worse than me. Bill looks up from his pad. My wife and her lawyer turn and stare at the building storm clouds hovering between us. This has apparently become interesting.

In a loud clear voice, which startles even me, I hear words start to pour out of my mouth. I'm excited to find out what I'm going to say. "Do I want to hear that woman read statements from my daughters that have been engineered by a lawyer to melt my insides? No, of course not. However, much like a cutter finds inner peace through razor blades and blood-letting, or a pig seeks out excrement to roll, so too can I not resist having my guts publicly torn out and trod upon. And so, YES, I contest. I contest them freezing my bank accounts. I contest them kicking me out of my garage. And I contest my wife having sole custody of my children. Read their statements. Do your worst. I contest."

Fin. What a soliloquy. I look at the stenographer to make sure her whirring fingers captured all my brilliance. I'm sure this case will be studied in law school classrooms all across America.

Bill drops his pen and stirs to life. "Your Honor, may I have a word with my client?"

The judge nods. Bill pulls me closer, places his hand over the side of our faces to hide the conversation and whispers aggressively into my ear, "Joel, what the *hell* was that?" He's trying to control himself, but I can feel little flecks of his spit stick to the side of my face.

I look at him, raising my eyebrows innocently. "What?"

"You can't talk like that here. I can't defend you if you're going to keep losing it in front of the judge. All the other crap with the drugs and the cat is bad enough. You're making my job extremely difficult if not impossible." He pulls back from my face and searches my eyes for some sign of understanding.

I feel a tap on my right shoulder. Kurt has made his way to the first row of seats and is leaning over the rail. I push away from Bill, turn my back to the judge and tilt towards Kurt's mouth. He leans over further, lips so close they tickle the delicate hairs around my ear. I feel a jolt of electricity pass through my body. He pauses, breathing softly, air faintly pushing in and out of his mouth, his proximity and familiarity is almost erotic. We make eye contact and he rasps, "I don't know why, I'd rather be dead than cool." That makes sense in a way that few things have lately.

"Joel!" There is a panic in Bill's voice now. He's staring at me, mouth agape. The room has adopted a similar wide-eyed look to Bill and everyone seems very interested in what I'm doing. I've got them wrapped around my finger now, hanging on every word.

I pull forward away from Bill. "Your Honor, please forgive the in-artful way in which I just expressed myself. As a wise man once said, 'give me liberty or give me death' or something. I wish to continue contesting the issues presented by my wife."

I take note that the judge appears to have completely lost interest in whatever was on the screen in front of him; such is the gravitational pull of my plea. Bill slumps in his seat. Kurt settles back and resumes scratching away in his notebook.

I look up to the judge. He takes a breath and holds my gaze. "Mr. Peterson, in light of the extremely erratic behavior you have displayed today and over the past month, I am very confident all of the steps outlined by Mrs. Peterson's counsel are in fact necessary as a safeguard for your children, and I do not need to hear their statements in order to rule so. However, for the sake of ensuring we have a complete record, I am going to require they be read aloud and included in the transcript of the proceedings. Also, to be frank, I hope inside of you there lies a shred of decency which may be shocked back to life. Counselor, you may proceed."

I look over at Mary. Fat, wet tears are streaming down her cheeks again. Wrecking her day continues to be a skill of mine. We haven't had a word pass between us since I ran over that cat, which is probably a good thing; the words we had been in the habit of exchanging before were not the nice ones.

Mary liked the money I earned and the lifestyle it afforded, but she did not like me. The contempt started gradually and built up bit by bit like plaque on teeth. I saw it happening but didn't care enough to try and brush it away. There isn't any singular moment I care to specifically point to; it just seemed like the minutia of the day-to-day wore her down. Before I knew it, the slime turned our marriage yellow, then black and rotten.

For months she watched me, waiting for any excuse. I suppose she was looking for lipstick on my collar or perfume on my shirt, any sorry cliché. In turn, I recognized this and measured my steps carefully. It was a fun game we played. Her constantly looking for tangible proof I was a scum bag, and me pretending I was unaware of her suspicions.

As the years passed in our marriage, I withdrew further into myself emerging only occasionally like a passive-aggressive turtle content to nip and then retreat back into my shell. The solution to my malaise never seemed to be a fuck-around with a girlfriend. Mary needed some catalyzing event to justify ending the charade. I just enjoyed our poisonous back and forth. It was easy for me to pretend I was the normal one, that all our problems were in her head. Playing oblivious to her misery made her even more frustrated. I felt like my life existed only from the outside. At some point I stopped feeling anything. I was experiencing my life like someone flipping through a photo album.

Here's me tucking Ollie into bed and giving her a kiss—classic Dad pose.

Here's me teaching Philly how to ride a bike just like my ancestors.

Here's me chopping carrots for dinner while Mary tries to pretend I don't exist.

I became incapable of experiencing genuine feelings in the moment. I participated in family life only to catalogue the moment and move on. I was checking the boxes of chores expected from a husband and father. If it wasn't photographed or video-taped, then for all I knew or cared the moment never existed. Everything was fleeting. I watched the girls pass through my life, here one minute, gone on the wind the next.

Observing my life became an easier existence. I didn't want another woman or a different family; I was winning with complacency. Then I ran over that damn cat right in front of Philly and Ollie and genuine feelings broke in and started wiping their shit-stained shoes over the glossy, plastic charade I had constructed.

We adopted Friskers from a no-kill shelter six months before I ended him with a well-placed tire. He was the girls' first pet. They couldn't get enough and heaped attention on him. His existence in my universe bothered me from the first day. I never allowed myself to examine the issue deeply enough to pinpoint the reason, but if I'm being honest, it may have been that it gave the girls a target for their affection, chipping away at the comfortable emotional zombification I had infected my family with. Mary quickly noticed how much it bothered me and encouraged their doting, turning the tide of our cold war. I began looking for any opportunity to do him in.

One day on the way to work, I saw Friskers lazily curled up in the early morning sun sleeping in the driveway right in the middle of everything, oblivious in the way only a cat can be. Full of hurt, I floored the Porsche and squished the orange, tabby fuck. The top was down, and when I saw his flattened carcass, I let loose a primal yelp, a sound that thousands of years ago would be familiar to any caveman striking a deathblow to a saber-tooth tiger.

Of course, lost to me in the frenzy of my murder were the girls. They stood twenty feet away, waiting for the school bus, watching it all. No amount of PCP will be able to wipe away the memory of the looks on their faces. I shifted the car back into park and tried to summon words. My mouth opened but my tongue was too dry to speak, and I quickly closed it again.

I watched as the quiver began in their necks, then moved into their jaws until tears streamed down their faces. I saw pure unadulterated hatred overtake their eyes. Even though they were years apart, in their anger and grief they were twins. Philly, being the good big sister that she is, recovered first and ran inside to get Mary. Ollie continued watching me in a boiling rage. The emotions were messier than the smear of cat on the driveway. I had made a life of wrapping everyone around me in plastic, but all it took was killing that dumb cat to break down all the barriers and drag me into the mud.

Running over that cat was a compulsion more powerful than sex with a beautiful stranger; it was the mistake I couldn't resist. The trap I couldn't dodge. Mary filed divorce papers the next day. I've been in the garage reduced to a casual observer of my family ever since. Now through a proxy I get to hear my daughter speak to me again.

The lawyer shuffles through some papers in front of her, clears her throat and stands up. Mary looks down at her lap and dabs at her cheeks with a wadded-up tissue. I wonder if this is hard on her because she feels bad for me or is this just the normal way to react to this kind of thing?

When the godfather of grunge starts speaking to you from beyond the grave, you can no longer be considered a good judge of what is normal.

"Your Honor, I would like to enter the following sworn statement by Olivia Peterson onto the record."

"Yes, Counselor, proceed."

My name is Olivia Peterson and I am nine-years-old. I live in Falmouth, Maine, with my mom and sister. My dad has been living in our garage. He used to be an okay dad, but now he is mean. He gives mean looks to my mom and pretends not to see me and my sister.

One day when we were waiting for the bus, I watched my dad kill our cat, Friskers. He hit Friskers with his car and then seemed really happy about it. I noticed right away how happy he looked because my dad never looks happy anymore, but he had a big mean smile when he saw he had killed Friskers. It was awful. There was blood all over our driveway, and it made me and my sister and my mom very sad. I don't want my dad to live in our garage anymore. He is not nice.

Sincerely,

Olivia J. Peterson

Ollie writes with an impressive clarity. I wonder what the letter sounded like before the lawyers cleaned it up. She said I used to be an "okay dad;" it's touching she thought of me in that way. It's more credit than I give myself. This is another reminder she's growing quickly. It seems like only yesterday she was incapable of delivering a spoonful of applesauce from the cup to her mouth without dropping most of it on her lap. Now she's writing letters analyzing the finer points of our family dynamics.

"I've heard enough, thank you, Counselor. Mr. Peterson, before I make a decision here, is there anything you would like to say?" the judge asks.

I take my time while pondering this question and take stock of my surroundings. Kurt has left the building again. There is no one else besides the judge who will look back at me. I feel like a lunatic.

Finally I respond, "No, Your Honor, I think this has been quite enough for one day."

The judge rolls his eyes and looks down from his throne while delivering his ruling. "Very well. Mr. Peterson, in light of the erratic behavior you have displayed inside this courtroom and the dangerous way with which you are apparently conducting your life outside of it, I have little choice but to act in the best interests of your wife and daughters. As such, I am ordering a freeze on all your bank accounts and credit cards as well as issuing an order of protection prohibiting you from being within two-hundred feet of your family at any time. In addition, as requested, two-hundred thousand dollars shall be moved from the joint checking account into an account solely under control of Mrs. Peterson."

Bill avoids all eye contact with either one of us. Should I presume the $50,000 deposit I signed over in the hospital has been spent and without a way to access the rest of my cash, I am to be left unrepresented? He stares silently at his yellow legal pad. I nudge him with an elbow to get his attention. He looks up sheepishly. Apparently, I am his first client to have a psychotic break with reality in a courtroom or something.

I whisper harshly into Bill's ear, "What about my business accounts? He can't shut down my office too."

Bill sighs audibly and rolls his eyes. His head drops as he tries to compose himself. One carefully placed lock of hair breaks free from the pack and folds down over his forehead. He just wants this and me to go away. One more deep breath and Bill finally stands pushing his chair back as he does. "Your Honor, as you know my client has significant assets tied to his dental practice. This business supports numerous employees and owns several bank accounts which are necessary to support its continued operations. Despite, the admittedly ... umm ... bizarre behavior exhibited by my client today, it would be excessive to keep him from making a livelihood." Bill seems to almost believe what he is saying.

Without hesitation, the judge answers, "The financial disclosures from each party show Mr. Peterson has accumulated very substantial assets. My foremost concern at this juncture is the preservation of these assets for the benefit of his children. So despite the unfortunate and unintended consequences for his employees, I have little choice but to place a hold on his practice's accounts as well. Furthermore, pending a forensic audit of Mr. and Mrs. Peterson's assets, I am going to require Mr. Peterson immediately relinquish his keys to his dental practice and refrain from entering the premises unless accompanied by a police officer."

He pauses and then continues, "I realize my ruling is harsh and may have unintended collateral damage on his innocent employees; however, in light of the very *criminal* activity which Mr. Peterson has engaged in, I feel it is the only way to protect his family from further damage. At this point, Mr. Peterson," he says looking directly at me, "you have proven yourself to be unsuitable for even the smallest sliver of trust."

Seemingly satisfied, my highly-paid advocate sits back down and resumes studying the intricate doodles he has etched across his legal pad. Bill does not seem interested in keeping his client from becoming destitute; without money or any prospects to acquire more, I no longer possess the requisite leverage to maintain his attention. This hearing is rolling down the mountain like an avalanche of bad news. I'm all out of ideas on how to stop the momentum.

The judge isn't done yet, "Mr. Peterson, I hope you have taken copious mental notes during this hearing. My ruling is quite serious. I want to make it extremely clear; I do not believe you are currently in any condition to be prodding people's gums with sharp objects. Nor would it be in anyway appropriate to allow you continued unfettered access to the drugs necessary to run a proper dental practice. If you are seen entering or in the vicinity of your office, it shall be treated as a direct violation of this court order and you are to be immediately placed into police custody. Is that clear?" The judge stops and waits for me to answer.

Without any other options, I nod in the affirmative. This seems to satisfy him. The judge acknowledges me with a "Humph," glances at the bailiff, turns and exits back into his quarters.

Very suddenly I seem to be without employment, without money, without shelter and without family. I have lived all my adult life full of *withs*. This development of *withouts* is startling. I slide the casts off my wrist and leg and place them on the table in front of me.

I feel lightheaded; my vision bursts into stars and my left hand starts to tingle.

I think these are the symptoms of a stroke.

I am a doctor.

I am going to have a stroke. I know this because I am a doctor.

I am having a stroke.

I am a dentist with very few life skills.

I think my nose is bleeding.

I can't believe it; I'm definitely having a stroke, how exciting.

Sitting patiently in my chair, I wait for the stroke to kill me in front of Mary. She should have to watch this, it's only fair.

The sensation builds and spreads into both hands and feet. Maybe this isn't a stroke; too many things are tingling at once.

I always assumed dying would be more interesting than this.

Everyone is standing and rustling their papers around. Apparently this hearing is over. I expected the judge to conclude the festivities with something more dramatic than a "Humph," like hammering his gavel or something. There is a low murmur throughout the room as people exchange pleasant small talk and pick up their belongings. Everyone is blissfully oblivious to the ruins with which I have been left. I hope this stroke hurries up and kills me before everyone leaves the room. It's sort of pointless to die if no one notices.

Mary and her attorney leave the room first. I stare at them as they exit, but neither one makes eye contact with me. She seems happy. Dammit.

Bill finishes sweeping miscellaneous papers into his briefcase and stands up to walk out of the room.

I get up and follow Bill out only because I don't know what else to do and it seems like a better option than sitting here forever. Also, I want to catch up to Mary in the parking lot so she has to watch me die.

Woozily, I chase him through the innards of the courthouse, uncomprehending of the route he takes to accomplish our flight. From behind, I have a chance to study Bill's carefully manufactured hair. It's combed from front to back and finished with a plastic flourish right above his neck. His one runaway lock carefully tucked back into place. From this angle, it's easy to see his slicked back hair covers an expanding bald spot. Hundreds of tiny dandruff flecks dot his dark mane, caught up in the hair gel like bugs in amber. He notices me following him over his shoulder and picks up the pace. Soon we are outside. My left foot is still numb. I wonder if I have enough to at least fake the stroke.

Mary is pulling out of the parking lot as we exit the building. Again she avoids eye contact. I watch her tail lights as her SUV pulls away. There is a distance opening up. For years I thought I was winning the battle of wills, that my stubbornness was impenetrable and perfect, but it's apparent now I have lost. She has escaped me.

I flex both of my hands repeatedly, but the tingling won't subside. I may throw up.

Bill is taking his coat off at his car. He lays it neatly in the trunk and closes it as I approach him. He looks at me sideways and says, "Tough break in there today, not a lot I could do. Especially with you talking to imaginary friends in front of the judge. Kind of tied my hands." Done packing his stuff into the car, Bill sighs. The fire he had on the day Friskers' head popped off is gone.

I've never been a religious man, but nevertheless I pray for a stream of projectile vomit to spew forth from my gut soaking him in loneliness and stomach bile. We both wait for a second, him to see if I have anything to say for myself, me to see if I can materialize some serious puke. Nothing. No smiting.

Bill opens the driver's side door and pauses again to look me in the eye before ambling in. "Take care of yourself, okay?" It's not really a question.

He ducks his head into the car, turns it on and pulls away. I am alone again squeezing my hands open and closed, open and closed.

I know intuitively it is a beautiful day; the early-summer sun sits high in the sky and a gentle breeze ruffles the new leaves on the trees. The streets are alive with happy people defrosting from a long winter, yet inside me a blizzard is building. Cold wind, driving snow, and freezing organs make rational thought all but impossible. Despite the season on the outside, a shiver rises from deep inside and passes through my body rattling bones. This must be what a death rattle feels like.

I see Kurt sitting on the guardrail, leaning back with his eyes closed and arms crossed soaking in the sun. Absent of any better options, I shuffle towards him. Hunched over and miserable every step feels like agony. A casual observer would have trouble discerning which one of us was the ghoul back from the dead after a shotgun blast to the face. He opens one eye when I get close and looks at me.

"Just you and me I guess," I say hopefully.

Kurt closes his eye, inhales deeply, holds it and concentrates on the sun washing over his face. Exhaling he says, "All alone is all we are."

CHAPTER TEN
Eat My Shame

THIS ALL SEEMS VERY ODD. Maybe I should ask Smiley to turn on the siren and the flashers. I kind of like the idea of being driven back into my wife's neighborhood, my old neighborhood, like a dangerous criminal.

Maybe if I start rattling the cage in the back seat of the cruiser and swearing at him, he'll put me in cuffs.

Maybe if I spit on him, he'll hit me in the face, chip my teeth, bloody my lip and blacken my eye.

Maybe if I kick at him, he'll drag me out of the car cuffed and beat me in the middle of the road while my wife, daughters and neighbors watch.

Maybe if I can manage to slip the cuffs under my feet, I'll get the jump on him and wring his neck.

Maybe he'll have no choice but to shoot me in self-defense

and hide my body in the sandbox with Friskers.

The daydream is tantalizing.

Smiley pilots the cruiser into a left turn and pulls into my former driveway. He takes a glance at the house then turns around and speaks through the cage in the backseat, "All right, your family is out of the house for the next hour. We'll go into the garage and pack up what you need. We will not be going into the main house. If there are items in there you need, you'll have to put them in writing and your lawyer can discuss it with your wife's attorney."

"That won't be necessary. I have nothing left in the house," I reply.

Smiley pauses, then adds, "Also, don't bring anything that can't fit in the cruiser. Let's keep this to the essentials, okay?"

He looks at Jorgensen and nods. Jorgensen sighs and hefts himself out of the passenger's side gut first. He opens the back door of the cruiser and lets me out. A thick bead of sweat has already formed on his forehead. "Let's get on with it then," Tubby says, holding the door open.

Smiley is already out of the car and standing by the door of the garage waiting for me to unlock it. He has his hands in his pockets and looks bored. He finds me less interesting since I conceded our tête-à-tête in the hospital room. It must be true that every great hero needs a worthy nemesis. I'm just the B-storyline to him at this point.

A truck drives slowly by taking note of the squad car and then the three of us. It's Terry Gross. I wave as he passes. Terry is a plumber and the only blue-collar person left in our neighborhood. He's been living here longer than anyone else. His fleet of vans seem out of place amid the sea of foreign sports cars and SUVs masquerading as practical family transportation.

I have always gone out of my way to be nice to Terry, as if acceptance by someone who still makes an honest living with his hands somehow validates me as more than two-hundred pounds of white meat that would die quickly and violently in the wild.

If the world's monetary systems collapse, what will people value more: clean teeth or the ability to shit indoors?

Terry clearly sees my wave but doesn't return the greeting. I guess word gets around.

I unlock the door pulling my stiff left leg behind me; Smiley and Jorgensen follow me upstairs into the apartment. It smells bad—musty and rotten. The girls must not have come up here since my accident. Surveying the sparse surroundings, I try to remember exactly why it was important to come back here. I can't imagine I actually need or want any of this stuff. Nothing up here is survival gear. My priority is high value stuff that can be quickly liquidated but fits in the back of a squad car. This is a short list.

Smiley walks around the apartment with his hands in his pockets, stopping occasionally to casually flip through magazines or examine photos. Jorgensen perches himself in the kitchen and leans heavily against the counter.

I pull a black backpack from the closet and begin picking through the rubble of my life. My iPad and charger are lying on the kitchen table. Those should have some sort of resale value. I place them in the bag.

Next, I head back to the bedroom closet and take my Armani suit off the rack. There's no reason to take up valuable space in the backpack so I put the suit on over the t-shirt and sweats I'm wearing. The suit reminds me that a Rolex and pretty decent collection of shoes are both in the main house; too bad, those would have flipped quickly. The thought of asking Bill to ask permission to go back inside to get them is too nauseating to stomach.

The TV is too big to take and probably too old even to pawn. Maybe some crackhead would pay for it? It's not worth the fight.

I look past Smiley and survey the kitchen for anything of value. The microwave or the toaster oven? The toaster is clean and small. The microwave slowly gives you testicular cancer. Toaster it is. I should be able to pull at least $20 for it.

Jorgensen watches as I cram the toaster oven into the backpack and sling it over my shoulder. The fat bastard looks amused. He strikes me as the type of sick fuck who sits around all day in a roach-infested apartment watching Faces of Death and Al-Qaeda beheading videos while eating cheese from a can.

This is what I've come to. Even fat, ugly, stupid, unambitious Jorgensen looks at me and thinks, "Well, at least I'm not that guy."

I scan the room again searching for anything with even a modicum of scrap value. I wonder if Smiley would stop me from pulling the copper out of the walls. Technically, I still own this mess. Truthfully, I have no idea what's behind the drywall or how to get it out. I'd probably kill myself trying.

Smiley rifles through a bowl sitting on the counter and holds up a set of keys. They are smartly labeled "office" and "storeroom."

"Are these your only set?" he asks.

Somehow, besides the ones kept by the girls who open up the office in the mornings, they are. I nod and Smiley slips the keys into his pocket.

Stepping past both cops, I open the door and head into the

apartment's cramped three-quarter bath. Kurt is standing in front of the mirror shaving. Surprised, I quickly move into the room and forcefully shut the door behind me. Kurt's only wearing some loose-fitting, plaid boxers. His shirt and pants are draped carefully over the shower stall. I watch mesmerized as he painstakingly pulls a razor against the grain over the three-day stubble on his neck. With the razor in his left hand, his right carefully navigates the taut skin like the neck of a guitar, guiding it across each hair, plucking them one-by-one, then back into the hot running water from the faucet. I watch in the mirror as his eyes shift to me standing in the threshold. His fingers continue their march across his face without missing a beat.

"How did you get here?" I ask.

His attention turns back to his face and he shrugs. It was a stupid question. How did *I* get here? The last time I saw him in the parking lot outside of the courthouse I thought I was having a stroke. Looking back, that may have been a rather brash diagnosis; the tingling and lightheadedness must have been symptoms of a massive panic attack. Smiley and Jorgensen found me sprawled face first in the grass crying softly.

These are confusing times we live in.

I don't know if they were always planning on picking me up at the courthouse or if the police station got a call about some lunatic talking to a guardrail, bothering innocent taxpayers, and they put two and two together. I guess it doesn't matter.

The way they herded me into the back of the car was almost tender like how they would handle an old man with Alzheimer's after some concerned citizen reported him walking down the middle of a freeway thumbing for a ride with shit in his pants. At first their compassion made me cry harder until I recognized the pity in Smiley's eyes, then my heart hardened into cold, steely hate.

They already knew the address.

They already knew about the restraining order.

They already knew Mary and the girls weren't home.

I sat in the back all the way home silently gnashing my teeth and stewing. I haven't seen Kurt since the parking lot, yet here he is again. Cycling through when I need him the least.

Still his presence is intoxicating. With him standing in front of me in my bathroom using my razor, I can't find it in me to hate. Out of everyone he has chosen me. With the door closed, the hot water from the tap is starting to steam the mirror up, distorting my view of his face. He continues shaving with a skill borne of nimble fingers unencumbered by the diminishing returns of the mirror.

I clear my throat in a way meant to convey authority but instead sounds like a pubescent boy trying to preempt his voice from squeaking in front of the girl he likes.

"What are you doing here?" I ask barely managing the force necessary to get the words up my neck and out past my lips.

He ignores my question and continues working through the whiskers on his neck. Two more upstrokes and he pauses, turning his chin left then right, inspecting. His eyes go back to me in the mirror and he sighs, clearly upset that I am still behind him waiting for an answer. Pulling the hand towel off the rack, Kurt finally turns and looks at me. Eye to eye. Pupil to pupil.

Molecules rub against each other seeking out ions with the same electrical charge. The chaos erupting inside me at a cellular level makes the hairs on my neck stand up. Fireworks shoot out of my fingertips. It has been weeks since I have taken any PCP, but I feel the same high. Somewhere deep inside me, I know something is wrong. That this is some sort of fantasy I should overcome, but it's easy for me to feel like that on the inside, insulated from the full power of the experience. Nearer the surface is nothing but an urge to drink deeply of him and submit. Submit, give-in, participate, cast-off. DO IT. The pull coming from him: illusion, ghost, cadaver, whatever, is beyond my ability to resist anymore.

"Teenage angst has paid-off well. Now I'm bored and old," Kurt says matter-of-factly.

His voice has a sing-song quality. He speaks with an easy confidence like there are no troubles in the world which can't be remedied. I want that voice inside my head. I need guidance. Back in my garage overlooking the house I built for the family that doesn't want me anymore I know I am vulnerable, but I don't care. There is a wisdom to that voice; it's the one that wormed its way into a generation's subconscious, scaring parents while depressing and exhilarating their kids. A Pied Piper emptying wallets and filling heads with angst until the sheer force of his siren song drove him mad, crashing headfirst into heroin, then into a bullet through his skull.

Where would the steel necessary to resist this come from? I tried it my way and woke up with a cast on my leg, no car, no money, no job, no family; now I'm ready to embrace change.

"What should I do?" I ask. Even off the drugs my head feels like a merry-go-round. How did things deteriorate so quickly?

Kurt seems bored by me already. He sighs and answers apathetically, "Just because you're paranoid, don't mean they're not after you." As if it was the most obvious thing in the world.

Smiley raps on the door with his knuckle startling me.

"Everything okay in there? We have a limited amount of time. Have to be in and out before your family comes home." He sounds impatient.

"Uh yeah, I decided to quickly shave. I'll be out in a second," I call back through the door.

Kurt shuts off the faucet, pulls on his shirt and steps into the shower to hide. I close the curtain around him, then open the door. Smiley and Jorgensen are both standing outside the bathroom looking at me. I can't help but notice they can't help but notice that there is still dark stubble on my cheeks.

I choose to ignore my obvious lie and push past them towards the couch collecting the backpack with the toaster oven haphazardly sticking out of it. Pausing to scan the apartment one more time; it occurs to me I may not be in this place again for a long time. There is a framed picture of the girls on the counter. For a second, I consider sticking it in the bag making a show of being a caring father for the cops, but space is too precious.

Even from ten feet away I can hear Jorgensen's rasping breaths as he putters aimlessly around the room. Pulling oxygen down his fat throat apparently requires more effort than food.

My contempt is distracting.

I have so much stuff and so little of it is worth anything. What have I done with my life? A thought occurs to me—not only should I be poaching items of value but considering the circumstances and the habits I have recently acquired of toeing the line between life and death, it would behoove me to remove items that could result in post-mortem embarrassment. The thought of Mary or the girls rifling through my stuff confronting my darkest secrets, even dead in the ground, sends a shiver up my spine.

Sometimes we must be our own publicist.

I look around the small seedy apartment; nothing stands out as needing immediate disposal. Perhaps I've become too accustomed to my own filth and debauchery. I continue scanning the room until my eyes fall on the closet next to the cabinets in the kitchenette. The closet of secrets.

I can't rationalize why this matters so much; my dignity has not been well-guarded as of late, but picturing the girls combing through the intimate details of my life, of who I really am feeds the compulsion. I have to scrub and control the narrative while I still can.

Panic grows in my throat and the closet begins throbbing like a tell-tale heart. I need to get Smiley and Jorgensen out of here. This could be my last chance.

Both flat foots are still standing in the corner outside of the bathroom casually watching me disintegrate. Gathering all my remaining willpower I drag my eyes off the door of the closet and force them to continue to scan the room, trying to be cool. I clear my throat and choose the words carefully swallowing back the dread and manage to muster, "Umm, I need a few minutes alone." That sounds perfectly reasonable.

"Why?" Smiley asks.

"I have personal matters up here I need to address." Personal could be anything. Everything is personal. This is not suspicious.

"Like what?" he asks.

"It's personal as I just said," responding aggressively. Okay, so it is a little suspicious. Alright, *very* suspicious. That doesn't matter so much right now as just getting them out of the apartment. I can hear the closet door rattling on its hinges. Sweat starts slowly seeping out of my armpits. Soon I'll smell like Jorgensen. This is my last chance.

Smiley steps forward, curiosity piqued. "Mr. Peterson, of course you understand the circumstances around this request, right?"

The condescension is layered thick in his voice like a kindergarten teacher explaining to some booger-eating kid how to clean up for the hundredth time. I choose to treat it as a rhetorical question and refuse to answer.

Seeing there will be limited class participation during this lesson, Smiley smiles then continues, "What I mean is, Mr. Peterson, you have had a very exciting month and are facing some potentially serious drug-related charges." He pauses and looks at Jorgensen who nods. "So we'll give you ten minutes alone to get your affairs in order, but we will search you before you get back in the car, and if necessary, we'll perform a *very* thorough search back at the station. Do you understand?"

We stare at each other and wait. His patience insists this one is not a rhetorical question. I nod.

"Mr. Peterson, I want to hear you confirm our understanding," he commands, his voice strained.

We're a long way from the hospital meeting when I thought this rookie could be strong-armed. My will grows less indomitable every day. "Yes, I understand. You're going to check inside my butt back at the station."

Smiley rolls his eyes. "No funny stuff."

I can't tell if this is a statement or a question but for the sake of efficiency I answer affirmatively, "No funny stuff."

Smiley looks at his watch. "Alright. Ten minutes. We'll meet you outside. And remember don't take anything that can't fit in the cruiser." He tilts his head at Jorgensen and they move towards the door.

I keep it cool until the lock clicks into the jamb. Then my lungs deflate and my breath comes pouring out in a violent rush.

The door beckons. Moving across the room, my hand finds the knob and exposes the worst of myself to the light. Set on the floor is a plastic penis pump and giant glass butt plug purchased in a moment of desperate exploration. I pick them up and place them on the counter. I was high when I bought them, but I never found the appropriate mix of substance to supply the courage to use them. It's embarrassing but at least it's not criminal. On the top shelf are five years of tax returns and books cooked to grossly underreport the income I earned. It would require no more than a cursory examination for Mary or her attorney to understand my fraud. I remove the stack and place them next to the pump and plug on the counter.

Kurt shuffles over and without a word places the paper in the sink, takes out his lighter, then starts burning the entire pile. I'm not sure what good that does in terms of hiding evidence, but nonetheless watching the flames lap up the paper feels cathartic. He bends down and lights a cigarette on the flames and drags deeply, letting the smoke billow out of his nose.

I watch him flabbergasted; I have never been that cool in my entire life. After a few minutes, the flames die down and Kurt turns the faucet on washing the ashes down the drain.

Without looking up he grabs the sex toys. I open my mouth to explain, but I don't know what to say. He doesn't seem interested anyway. I watch paralyzed as he jams the plug into the pump then pushes them into the garbage disposal. Next, he rifles through the cabinets pulling out a large metal pot. Placing the pot over the pump he flicks on the switch above the sink. We listen in silence as the disposal eats away. The pot dings loudly as small chunks of plastic and glass fly around underneath it. The disposal whirs fiercely as it eats my shame; thankfully its appetite is immense.

With one hand securing the pot, Kurt takes out the cigarette and lets loose another enormous cloud of smoke. Some of the pressure inside my guts releases as the narrative gets scrubbed. This is the first kindness anyone has paid me in months. I can't remember ever being so grateful for anything.

We make eye contact as he raises his eyebrows and nods his head back to the closet. Time is running out. The escorts are still waiting outside and there is still more legacy polishing to be done.

I tuck back in and push through the old CDs and DVDs that are stacked on the floor—more ghosts whispering to be released back out into the world. I ignore them and dig until I find an old, tattered box. I fish it out setting it on the kitchen counter. It's full of drawings, cards and knick-knacks from the girls, little projects they made in pre-school for Father's Day or birthday cards shakily lettered under the guidance of Mary. Some of the bigger ticket items already adorn a wall in my office, a show for anyone that enters that I am a sentimental family man getting through the day only by surrounding myself with little reminders of my darling family. It helps me keep the hygienists under control and tamps down any gossip about my personal life. That's most days. Other times, I really do understand the appeal of these sorts of things. Items are powerful talismans even if they represent the ideal, not the reality.

I flip through some of the stuff in the box, red construction paper hearts for Valentine's Day, a pair of cut-out handprints for Father's Day. Kurt looks over my shoulder as I shuffle through.

After going through everything, I pull out a family photograph of the four of us cut into a heart and pasted on a piece of folded white computer paper along with a handful of the girls' drawings. The photo I place on the nightstand directly next to the bed I never sleep in. The drawings I scotch tape up over the headboard and wall that borders the mattress.

I stand back and take stock of my work. It looks authentic. Like a man desperately missing his family. I can picture their faces when they finally come up here to clean up and are confronted by just how much I really care. How could they kick me out of my house, out of my garage and out of their hearts? The sympathy they are going to feel is almost enough to bring me to tears. This is good stuff; they won't be able to deny me forever.

I pick up the card one last time before I leave the room. It's four or five years old, I think. I'm holding the girls and Mary is behind me. Everyone is smiling broadly, including me. I look genuinely happy and so do they. I don't remember this day. I don't know who took the picture or where it was, but I look happy. Maybe I wasn't so bad.

I show the picture to Kurt. "Look at my face. I can't remember anything about this day but it really happened. This is photographic proof."

He takes the photo in his hands and studies it sadly. "Wish I had more opportunity. More chances to remember some things." He flips the card over and reads the inscription, then places it gently back on the nightstand, being careful to aim it directly towards the pillow.

We both look at the room one more time. It looks like a sad but innocent bachelor pad. It's perfect.

Shouldering the bag full of junk and wearing my best suit over sweats, I open the door and step out into the real world.

CHAPTER ELEVEN
A Good Boy

MY DEODORANT FAILS immediately as I step outside with the backpack over my shoulder, laden heavily with the toaster oven, the straps cut painfully into my shoulders. The suit over my clothes is suffocating. I find the two cops leaning against the cruiser chatting pleasantly about the Red Sox. There is no avoiding the relativity of the human experience. While one man is secretly force-feeding a garbage disposal his greatest shames, others are debating the finer points of bullpen usage in the American League East. The tables of life have turned on me.

Without breaking the stride of their debate, Jorgensen opens the cruiser's backdoor while Smiley blocks my entrance and motions for me to hand over the backpack. I let him take it and watch as he opens it and quickly runs through its contents. Satisfied, he hands it back to me and makes a move like he is going to pat me down, then thinks better of it and steps out of my path. I tumble into the backseat, relieving myself of the weight of the backpack and melt tiredly into the cushions. Smiley starts the car and pulls out of the gravel drive. Rocks clink loudly under my seat as the tires spray the undercarriage of the cruiser.

Silently, like a kid on a school bus for the first time, I watch out the back window as my driveway, then the house and finally my street fade out of view.

The cops don't address me. I listen while they debate whether Big Papi is finally washed up and the value of sabermetrics. I don't even know where they are taking me; no one has asked what I want. It doesn't matter anymore if they did ask; I wouldn't know what to say.

Once again, I find myself a mere passenger floating in the current like a jellyfish: spineless, directionless and hopeless. The car vibrates pleasantly as it delivers me to places unknown. I wish I was little and this was the back of my parents' station wagon. I don't want to be responsible for myself anymore. No one ever told me you could fuck up adulthood. If I had known it was the razor's edge I was walking, maybe I would have been more careful. Instead, I've made a mess of it all.

Somewhere underneath all the shit called adulthood there are core nuggets of goodness, but the nuggets are both blond and neither one of them like me. I don't think I have the tools to tunnel through the muck and get back the good in life.

Smiley and Jorgensen pull into the station. What joy. They back into a parking space, turn off the engine, then let me and my pack out of the back seat.

Standing by myself in front of a row of police cruisers, I look at them helplessly. Are you my father? Fuck.

Smiley watches my internal struggle and says, "Well, this is the end of the line. Do you have an address where we can find you?"

"No. Haven't really had a chance to think that far ahead," I answer honestly.

"Well, as you know there were some pretty serious substances in your body at the time of the accident. Nothing has been settled yet on how that issue is going to be handled. Until we give you the clear, I would highly advise you not to leave the state. Do you understand?"

I nod.

"Also, stay away from your family. If you see them out or recognize their car in front of a store, turn and walk the other way. Trust me, you don't want that kind of trouble."

No sir, I'll be a good boy.

Smiley stares at me with paternalistic sternness waiting for more than my inner monologue to acknowledge him.

"Right, got it. Walk the other way. Got it," I concede.

We stare at each other across the trunk of the cruiser. This is awkward.

"You're free to go," he says impatiently, like I am a stray dog he is trying to get to stop following him.

Maybe I could get arrested. I suppose it doesn't even have to be a violent crime. Perhaps I could whip it out and start peeing on the wheel of the car in front of them.

Prison seems scary. I'm probably not the prison-type.

There are other options. My mind has been making up a lot of shit lately. I would seem to be a fine candidate for the nut house. What would it take to get me into one of those fine institutions?

Maybe I should bite off Jorgensen's ear.

The prospect of this much freedom is paralyzing.

Smiley does all but shoo me away with his hand. Go on little bird, you're free. Fly away. Please. He and Jorgensen aren't quite dumb enough to turn their backs to me, but it is clear they are tired of my trivial issues.

I guess it is up to me to end this stand-off. Try and get locked up or unclip the wings and figure it out. I take one more long look at Jorgensen's ear; he rubs it self-consciously. Even from a distance, I can tell it's covered in hair like he's half Yeti or something. I bet the inside has never seen the clean end of a Q-tip. The thought of his blood in my mouth is almost enough to make me retch.

My time on earth has not prepared me for this moment. This feels like a tipping point or perhaps more aptly, a ripping point.

Everything I've done and everywhere I've been so far in life has been along a guided path. My parents saw me through the trials of puberty and into college. I stayed there as long as possible and then society had an easy, paint-by-numbers life laid out for me to follow: come back home, hang out a shingle, scrape teeth.

Easy, clean.

Now that path has disappeared.

I am hurtling back towards the earth at a startling speed.

I can smell my hair burning as I re-enter the atmosphere.

I am a tire fire of failure.

With no other appealing options, I slowly start shuffling away from Smiley and Jorgensen and into the abyss of the unknown.

CHAPTER TWELVE
Invisible

ON MY OWN with a toaster oven pulling down the pack slung over my shoulder, I move through the streets of Portland lost in thought. I'm at risk of swallowing my tongue if I think too far into the future. For now, the panic is packed away inside of me, safe in my stomach. If I let my guard down, it's ready to leap up my throat, into my head, and peel out of me in a sanity shredding scream.

It seems the only way to function is by limiting my thoughts to events easily controllable and no more than five minutes in the future. Thinking much beyond my next breath starts to darken the circles that have already formed in the underarms of this ridiculous Armani suit I had to wear. Taking this with me now seems like a comically bad idea especially if it's ruined with sweat before I have a chance to flip it.

I must stay focused on the present, step-by-step. Never before have I had to wonder where I was going to sleep, what I was going to eat, or what I was going to do to fill my time.

I pass invisibly through the crowds of downtown tourists with their flip-flops, stupid hats and oppressively-patterned shirts. Past the bars and crowded restaurants and down towards the docks. The only people who notice me are the various winos and drug addicts sprawled around the streets begging for change. They nod as I pass not bothering to ask me for anything. A few hungrily eye the toaster on my back. None of this is a good sign.

There is an ATM at the corner of Fore Street where all the bars are. I belly up to it and check over my shoulder to make sure none of the riffraff are making a move on me. None are. I take out my first debit card, insert it, punch in my PIN number and request $20. The machine hums softly as it considers my request and returns an obscenely red screen: "REQUEST DENIED, INSUFFICIENT FUNDS. WOULD YOU LIKE ANOTHER TRANSACTION?" There is over $100,000 in that account.

I start over again at the home screen and cycle through the rest of my debit cards with the same result. Next, I try cash advances from my armada of credit cards but all of those are denied too. Who says the wheels of justice grind slowly? When they really want to get something done, they are remarkably efficient.

I push away from the ATM and head over to the bank two streets over. It's my normal branch. They love me there, as they should. If a millionaire can't get preferential treatment in a bank, then something is seriously wrong. I walk through the doors, bypass the counter and head right into Rodney's office. He's overseen my accounts for the last three years. His chin is propped in his right hand while his left idly works the mouse, probably playing spider solitaire or some shit. I startle him as I cross the threshold of his tiny glass office and sit down in one of the two chairs that ring his desk. I dump my bag on the other and lean back looking at him.

"Uhh, can I help you, sir?" Rodney stammers.

"I certainly hope so, Rodney."

"Ahh, I'm sorry, do I know you?" he asks, his voice quivering.

"Joel Peterson."

He frowns and studies my face, brow furrowed. A light goes off somewhere behind his eyes and his eyebrows arch. "Mr. Peterson, I-I'm sorry. I didn't recognize you at first. You look ... ahh, are you okay?"

"No, I'm not all right. See this?" I ask, motioning towards the bag. "This currently holds all of my worldly possessions. And when I went to use my debit card just now, the ATM said my account had insufficient funds."

"Yes, actually I've been meaning to call you; it's good you came in." Rodney reclaims a bit of his composure. "Your accounts, all of them, have been frozen. Something to do with your divorce. We got this." He pulls out an official-looking piece of paper out of an open drawer and passes it across the desk to me. "Unfortunately, when we get one of those, there is nothing we can do even for our best clients."

I take the paper and pretend to study it closely as if I can really understand it. It doesn't matter. I know it's hopeless but I decide to press anyway. I pass the paper back to him.

"You don't understand. I need access to the money in that account."

"I'm sorry, Mr. Peterson, I wish I could help. You've always been a valued customer, but my hands are tied here."

"There has to be something you can do. Spot me a loan or move some money around. Be creative."

He sighs and leans forward on his desk. "I can give you fifty dollars, if that would help."

"What? Fifty dollars? I've funneled millions through this place." The tone of my voice is turning whiny. Begging a banker, pathetic.

"I'm sorry, fifty dollars is the best I can do. Any bigger discrepancy and they start to ask questions. We're federally regulated you know." He pulls back from the desk satisfied and watches me.

I sit back too and we have a staring contest. Neither one of us flinches. Finally, I break the silence. "Fine, I'll take the fifty dollars."

"Great!" he says, popping the desk lightly with his palm. "I'll be right back." Rodney gets up and walks over to one of the tellers. She hands him a bill. He comes back in and stands next to my chair. This must be my cue to leave.

I stand up as he passes me the bill then extends his hand for a shake. "You've always been one of my favorite customers. I don't doubt we'll overcome this little rough patch and be back in business with you soon."

I pocket the bill and take his hand begrudgingly. He pumps it up and down vigorously with a grin on his face, and with that I'm whisked past the tellers and back outside. This is what I get for using some podunk local banker. I should have opened an off-shore account managed by a blood-thirsty shark, like the ones I see in all the documentaries about when the economy crashed.

I move the bill to my wallet and make my way down to the benches that overlook the harbor, dropping the backpack at my feet.

Time to inventory the rubble of my life:

One used iPad with charger, value: $100

Two pair underwear, value: Nothing

Three pair white undershirts, slightly stained, value: Nothing

One blue pinstriped Armani suit, sweaty, value: $150

One white Cuisinart toaster oven, value: $25

One leather wallet with $50 in cash, a bunch of useless plastic and one black AMEX card, value: $50

Maybe I can sell the credit card as a novelty. I bet a hipster would pay $5 to ironically cut his cocaine with one of the world's foremost symbols of prestige and power.

Total: $330 in assets

What can $330 buy? How much are one-bedroom apartments in this town? Probably more than $330. How am I going to sell this shit? Should I just lay out a blanket on the street and start hawking? Is this what pawn shops are for? I think I saw a TV show about one once, but they seemed mostly interested in items with historical significance.

Is there a low-rent district around here where all the pawn shops are?

What am I supposed to eat?

Where should I buy food?

The panic is getting closer and closer to my throat. My breathing is becoming forced and ragged. These attacks are tiresome. There is no mistaking it for a stroke this time. I need to refocus on immediately executable tasks at hand. Taking a deep breath, I look around at my life laid out in front of me. It's still too much to process. I need some help. Someone needs to tell me what to do. Where is that fucking poet voice of a generation?

I hold my breath and concentrate my mind's eye on the steely-blue eyes, floppy blond hair and boyish good looks. I imagine him materializing next to me on the bench. I picture him hugging and gently rocking me as I cry.

Everything will be all right.

Everything will be okay.

We're going to find some money. We're going to make my family take me back. We're going to buy a new car. We're going to drill teeth again. This is just a bad dream; everything will be fixed. I open my eyes and exhale but the bench is empty; I'm still alone. My lungs deflate along with my will.

Someone needs to think this through for me. It will be dark soon and I need to figure out an option besides sleeping on the bench. A pawn shop is probably the best place to start. I'll bring this stuff to a pawn shop, rent a motel room, get some food and figure a way out of this mess.

Well shit, stupid. I do have more money—a lot more money—in cash. Enough money to solve all, or most of, these problems. Blood starts running back to my extremities. The terror retreats down my throat into the more manageable spot in the pit of my stomach. There is at least fifty grand in gloriously green $100 bills in the safe at my practice. Smiley and his fat partner Jorgensen pop back into my brain. My office is locked for the sole purpose of keeping me out. I need to break back into the office and reclaim what is mine.

I gather the goods carefully back into the pack. All my

worldly possessions. It's supposed to feel liberating, freeing myself from the shackles of my possessions. I don't own them, they own me, etcetera, etcetera, etcetera. Being left behind is not freeing, it's crushing.

Tyler Durden was full of shit; sticking feathers in your ass *does* make you a chicken. Without stuff we're just bags of bones drifting aimlessly. Our possessions give us the goals that keep us tethered to the earth. Without the drive to acquire, there would be no need to succeed and we would float away on a breeze. It's impossible to float away from a $10,000 Italian leather couch in the living room of an $800,000, five-bedroom, seven-bathroom Tudor. Those are the movers and shakers that matter. When they're missing, people take notice.

When will someone notice that I'm missing? There are only a few possibilities. Cindy and the rest of the women at the clinic will definitely notice when they try to get into work. They'll notice again when the payroll company tries and fails to debit from my frozen bank accounts. It seems unlikely any of them will be of much use.

Mary and the girls expect me gone and are seemingly unconcerned about where I go or what I do so long as I respect their two-hundred-foot cocoon. There is no other family to speak of and what little is around is taking Mary's side in all of this anyway.

The cops know roughly where I am and don't seem too bothered one way or another. The hospital scheduled a check-up for me at my primary care, but no alarms will go off when I no-show that appointment.

There are a few creditors. The Porsche and Mary's car are paid-off. There is a small mortgage on the house which Mary was always responsible for managing. Life insurance is paid quarterly and I bet Mary will make sure that is maintained. The strings connecting me to my life are frayed. I never figured they were this fragile.

The government will notice when I stop making any tax payments, but they're unlikely to mobilize a search and rescue party.

Someone, anyone, must have an idea of what to do. I look around hopefully, but there is still no sign of that greasy-haired, mumble-tone, god of rock and roll.

The day is getting gray. Looking out over the harbor, I can see storm clouds building from the south. It is going to be a cold and wet New England night. I need to find some place to weather the storm. This is turning into more than a metaphor.

I take one more look at the sky and then scan the park again: nothing except some seagulls and nervous-looking tourists. Everyone, bird and human, is watching the sky now. There is lightning in the distance and the rumble of thunder is faintly audible. The pages turn whether you want them to or not. Time to move on.

I take off the suit, carefully roll it like a joint and slip it into the backpack underneath the toaster. Mary used to pack my luggage like this to keep my clothes from getting creased. My execution is not as flawless as hers; I can already see where the wrinkles are going to form. I feel like a little kid.

There is no way around it, I feel bad for myself. It was nice to be loved. Perhaps I took some things for granted.

Perhaps, perhaps, perhaps.

This is no place for self-pity. That can come later. Self-pity right now is just going to get me extremely wet.

I pick up the pack and the toaster and move quickly back up

the hill away from the water and the tourist section, back into the heart of the city.

The rumbling in the distance is growing louder as I run-walk up the street. A bolt of lightning flares behind me. I count to fifteen M-I-S-S-I-S-S-I-P-P-I before the corresponding sound of the atmosphere ripping open catches up with me.

A middle-aged man wearing Teva's with socks, khaki shorts and a purple golf shirt stops with his wife under an awning and unfolds two large neon yellow parkas. I watch as they slip them over their heads. A cruise line's logo is emblazoned across the front. Tucked securely inside their brightly colored plastic, the couple now resembles trash bags full of lumpy nuclear waste. Somewhere a marketing director for Princess Cruises is shuddering involuntarily. There is no dignity to existence anymore.

Lightning strikes again; I make it to seven M-I-S-S-I-S-S-I-P-P-I this time. People are starting to scatter.

Up the hill I march past the restaurants and condos towards the last patches free of gentrification. From three blocks away I can see the neon gas burning in brightly-colored tubes like a trashy oasis blinking: "OPEN Old Port Pawn and Loan."

CRACK!

Thunder booms above me. The lightning sizzles simultaneously. Hairs on my arms and neck stand straight up. The smell of ozone fills my nostrils. The feeling is primal. Like a wolf, a caveman, or Bigfoot. A strong gust of wind rips between the buildings flattening the hair on my neck again. For a moment, I drop the self-pity and it feels exhilarating to be alive. Then the rain starts and my darkness resumes.

Sprinting the last three blocks, I am able to make it into the shop just as grape-sized raindrops start dotting the sidewalk.

When the door opens, a man behind the counter shifts his eyes up, greeting me with a gaze of indifference from underneath his formidable forehead. He has a thick beard and is wearing an unseasonably-warm flannel shirt. Without trying, he embodies the authenticity every hipster strives for. He eyes me, nods, then looks back down at the newspaper spread over the counter.

Time to dicker. I straighten the pack, gather myself and walk up to the counter.

He senses my approach and without looking up, out of the corner of his mouth asks, "Whatcha got, bub?"

I sling the pack up on the counter. The order I present these seems important. Should I lead with the best stuff and try to set the tone or sacrifice the shit to make the iPad look better?

I start with the toaster. It clatters loudly on the counter. The Beard eyes it suspiciously. "What else ya' got?" he asks, looking into the pack.

I see. He wants me to show all my cards at once. I realize now, too late, that this is a seasoned dickering professional. I am hopelessly overmatched.

Thunder booms outside rattling the shop's windows in their frames. The rain becomes torrential battering the windows in sheets. For a moment, we both stare silently outside as Mother Nature throws her hissy fit. The sound of water on glass is mesmerizing. The Beard clears his throat and breaks the spell. He nods at the pack again. Get on with it.

Next, I unroll the suit and try my best to smooth out the wrinkles. I leave the jacket lapel open so he can see the Armani label. It doesn't do much good.

Last out is the iPad and charger. I keep the underwear packed away.

Here it is, the tattered remains of my life. Do your worst, Beard.

"Ah, yeah guy, is that it?" he asks.

I nod affirmatively.

"Pawn or sell?"

I knew this question was coming because I saw it on that T.V. show. "Sell," I say with pride, showing I can hang with his vernacular. I am an old pro; this won't be as easy as you thought, Beard.

He picks up the suit and fingers it expertly. He turns the iPad over in his hand and pushes the button; the screen lights up. Bringing the toaster oven behind the counter, Beard plugs it in. He turns the dial to broil and watches as the coils heat up and glow. I am the purveyor of only the highest quality goods. Prepare to pay top dollar for these top shelf items, Shopkeep.

He snorts and unplugs the toaster. By his reaction, I can't tell if he is excited by the prospect of offering this oven in his shop. He's playing it close to the vest.

Rain pounds loudly on the window. Over my shoulder, I hear the door open and close as another lost soul takes refuge, but I stay focused on this tête-à-tête with Beard.

"I can give you twenty dollars for the oven, seventy-five for the iPad and fifty for the suit."

The customer walks behind me and heads to the guitar section.

I crack my knuckles reflexively. "I want thirty dollars for the oven, a hundred and fifty for the iPad and a hundred and fifty for the suit," I counter.

Behind me the other customer begins distractingly strumming an unplugged electric guitar. It twangs loudly reverberating throughout the shop.

The Beard considers my offer for a moment. "You can keep the oven for all I care, not worth a penny over twenty dollars to me. The iPad has a scratch on the screen, I can do ninety dollars. The suit, I'm not sure if I should even make an offer."

"That's a three-thousand-dollar suit," I plead.

"Uh-huh, I bet it was. Where'd ya get it? Ya steal it?"

"No, I bought it. Look, things haven't been great for me lately. I need some money, so I'm selling the suit. I haven't stolen anything ever." I blush a little bit at the last lie as at least a half-dozen instances of petty theft and larceny flash through my mind.

"Yeah well, sorry but your problems don't make your stuff more valuable. I'm at twenty dollars for the oven, ninety dollars on the iPad and ...," he holds the suit up against his body.

"Looks like a good fit," I say hopefully. My attempt at salesmanship feels pathetic.

I exhale as wind literally leaves my sails. My mind races again while cataloguing the stuff I left behind in the garage. My choices seem so foolish now. The best laid plans of mice and men, or something.

The Beard looks at me and frowns, then lays the suit back on the counter. He strokes his whiskers, puzzled.

Somewhere in the back the guitar player has plugged into an amp and is noodling loosely on David Bowie standards. The jagged opening riff of *The Man Who Sold the World* rings out through the shop. Over the din, I can hear the player garbling through the familiar lyrics.

As quickly as it started, the rain stops its pounding on the windows. I look over my shoulder. The guitar section is in a loft up a circular staircase. Kurt is sitting on an amp strumming the guitar and looking down at the Beard and me. He nods his head towards me. I turn back to the Beard who is still stroking his chin and staring at the suit. My presence is apparently unimportant to his decision-making process; it seems best I let him have some space to think. Besides, there are more important puzzles waiting for me in the guitar section.

"I'll just go look around for a bit while you think about it," I offer helpfully.

Kurt watches me as I climb the stairs towards him, never breaking rhythm with the guitar.

It feels like all the mysteries of existence are sitting in front of me wearing plaid and humming along with a guitar. His hair dips over his forehead clouding his view. I can't help myself as I reach over and tenderly push it away from his eyes. The now familiar electricity is coursing through my veins again. I know this is a trick of my mind, but the delusion is delicious. The experience of standing before him is too visceral. It's better than any drug I've ever taken. I feel alive again.

Are you supposed to be able to smell apparitions? Are delusions supposed to flinch when you touch them?

"Why did you come here?" my voice cracks. I'm a little afraid of what his answer will be.

Kurt stops playing the guitar but lets the last chord reverberate through the shop. When it stops ringing, he says, "I need an easy friend."

I look into his eyes and say, "Aren't you dead?"

He shakes his head affirmatively. "I lie in the soil and fertilize mushrooms."

"Am I dead too? Did I die when the Porsche went off the road?" I ask.

Kurt shrugs and starts strumming the guitar in his lap. Rage bubbles towards my surface again. I can't be ignored anymore. I bend down face to face with him and grab the collar of his shirt. The guitar falls out of his hands in front of the amp and sends a shrieking feedback loop throughout the shop. He reaches down to pick the guitar back up, but I don't let him. Tightening my grip on his collar I shake him back into eye contact. He feels frail like holding a bird.

"Am. I. Dead?" I try again, enunciating every syllable through gritted teeth. I'm not sure what I want the answer to be, but I am sure he knows.

He forgets the guitar. We stare at each other. The feedback loop keeps building on itself becoming more and more abrasive. Rational thought is virtually impossible. Sweat drips over my eyes and I shake him again.

"Hey man, what the fuck are you doing?" The Beard is standing in front of me. He unplugs the guitar from the amp and the screeching stops abruptly.

Beard takes two fingers and pokes me sharply in the chest. "You planning on buying that?"

I look around confused standing by myself in front of the squealing equipment. What the fuck is going on? My mind feels fuzzy like I was just teleported from another dimension.

"Don't fuck with my stuff, okay? I'll give you ten dollars for the suit. Take it or leave it, but I want your crackhead ass out of my shop pronto. Got it?"

I consider his offer. My hands are still out in front of me clutching only air, no flannel shirt. Nothing. Maybe I am dead. I let that thought marinate for a second.

I have to pee. I don't think you have to pee when you're dead.

"Fine, I'll take it," I reply, still disoriented.

"Good. Let's go finish the paperwork so you can get the fuck out of here." In his anger, the Beard has lost much of his homey-Maine charm.

We go back down the stairs and the Beard writes up a bill of sale. He raises his eyebrows when I give him the ritzy address where Mary lives. "I'm going to ask you one more time, is this stuff stolen?" he asks aggressively.

"No," I reply.

He takes a wad of bills out of his pocket and shakes his head as he counts out six twenties. "This is against my better judgement." He lays the money on the counter.

I study the bills and the wad that they came from. "I want a hundred and fifty for the iPad."

He sighs and reluctantly peels off another twenty from the pile. "Fine, but you have to leave now."

I sweep the money into my pack and head out of the shop. It is raining again. Within seconds I am drenched. I look up the street towards the hill and then down towards the ocean. A man without a country. All things considered, it seems like a better idea to take my rock and push it up the hill. Thunder cracks. The storm has moved a few miles north. I begin my trudge towards higher ground.

CHAPTER THIRTEEN

Perfect Spoons

THIS ROOM SMELLS like weed.

The bed smells like piss.

Or maybe it's the salmon-colored, wall-to-wall carpeting that is holding in the piss stench. I crinkle my nose and examine the scratchy, beige bedspread. I can't even imagine the horrors it has seen.

I hope it's the carpet.

The room is sparsely decorated: twenty-year-old TV in the corner, queen-sized bed, nightstand, a framed poster of famous artwork on the wall, bathroom stocked only with hand towels and a bar of soap.

Even at my worst while living in the garage I had thousand

thread-count sheets and TiVo. This, a literal piss-hole, was the best I could do without a working credit card.

I suppose I should try to look at all the positives: It's not raining inside. This isn't a hospital room or a jail cell and it only cost me thirty bucks for the night.

Actually, the hospital room was pretty nice. People were attentive to my needs; there was food and drugs. Maybe I should throw myself out of the window and see if I can re-break a leg. I have to be out by 11:00 a.m. tomorrow and I've already paid for the night. I should wait to throw myself out of the window until tomorrow at 11:01 a.m.

This room has shed a harsh light on the dead or alive debate. I'm definitely alive. I doubt I'm a good candidate for heaven and this room isn't bad enough to be hell. Fuck, maybe there is a purgatory.

Catholics seem too ridiculous to have been right about any of this shit.

Despite the piss smell, I take a seat on the bed and get a good scratch going. My beard is really filling in.

The storm has subsided, but the humidity has not and my clothes are still drenched. Even in a piss-shit-hole like this, the prospect of a hot shower is tantalizing.

There is a digital alarm clock on the nightstand next to the bed; it says 6:00. The girls are home from school. Probably working on their homework in the kitchen while Mary cooks dinner. When I was in the middle of it, I found the minutia and routine suffocating. It was the same thing every night with the only benchmarks of progress being the extra hair growing out of my ears and wrinkles deepening on Mary's face. The drugs helped take the edge off, numbing me to the routine. Now stone cold sober for—actually I'm not sure how much time has passed since the accident—well sober for a while, I long for the security of family life. Dads should be at home helping with algebra.

The sun has broken through the clouds outside, but it still feels dark in the room. I get off the bed and open the shades wider. It doesn't do much to part the din.

On the table holding the TV is the bag of necessities I bought at the 7-11 down the street. It cost me over $25 of my last $200. I take it over to the bed and dump the bag out on the comforter. I've taken inventory of my life more times in the past two days than I did in the previous forty years:

One king-sized Snickers candy bar

One pouch of mesquite-flavored turkey jerky

One cup of instant noodles

One pack of cheese Danishes for breakfast

A disposable razor

A toothbrush

A travel-sized toothpaste

The motel room cost $30 plus a twelve percent hospitality tax for a total of $33.60. Despite the label on the tax I don't find this room overly hospitable.

I open my wallet: five $20 bills, four $10 bills and ninety-four cents in change; that and a spread of pre-packaged salt and sugar bricks passing for sustenance are all I count for.

I wonder what Mary is cooking for dinner tonight. I've lost track of what day of the week it is. If it's Sunday, she's cooking burgers made from local organic free-range beef on gluten-free buns. On Mondays, she would make vegetarian fed chicken parmesan, crusted in imported panko bread crumbs over a bed of organic farfalle. Tuesday is pizza night with home-made crust, vine-ripened organic tomato sauce and nitrate-free pepperoni. Wednesday was line-caught haddock over locally sourced mashed russet potatoes and organic haricot-vert sautéed in cold-pressed, extra virgin olive oil. Thursday was Mary's "lighter fare" with grilled tofu over organic quinoa. Hippies helped end a war; hipsters added $75 a day to my grocery bill. Friday and Saturday were reserved for take-out from the same three places.

When I was in the middle of it, life with Mary seemed as sterilized as the organic food she insisted on cooking. I missed the spice of pesticides. If nothing else, cancer at least seems interesting, but now thinking about her set-in-stone meal plan just makes me nostalgic for the suffocation.

Tragedy is supposed to be part of the human condition. No matter how much money I had, it was impossible to scrub the sadness out of me. My outside spoke of exotic vacations, organic foods and luxury cars. My inside said everything sucks and everyone is an asshole. Lately my outsides have been more aligned with my insides. At least I'm finally living honestly.

Looking around the room: there is no fucking microwave. I eye the pile of food on the comforter like a starving dog; for some reason, I am ravenous for it.

Tearing into the first package, I shovel the jerky into my mouth with greedy fingers. It is incredibly salty. Canker sores open underneath my tongue after only four pieces. It doesn't matter, the chemicals and sodium combine with my saliva to rival the best steak I've ever had. At the end, I open the pack as wide as possible and funnel the scraps into my jaw. Tiny pieces of meat flood my mouth. I move them around with my tongue pressing them against the spots where I can feel the cankers forming. The nerves in my mouth jump all the way to my eyeballs making my teeth tremble. I imagine this is what a tick feels like when a lit cigarette is put to its bloodthirsty head—glorious.

Next, I rip open the Snickers and eat it in three bites. My mouth is gummed up with nougat and caramel. Pleasure neurons fire off in my brain, flooding me with good juju. Somewhere a food scientist must be touching himself.

The gooey mess coats between my teeth, pressing against all the soft spots in my enamel. In some ways, I owe everything I have to chemically engineered, addictive, acidic, poisonous garbage food like this. In this moment with a mouthful of sludge, it seems like a square trade. My life for your pleasure chemicals. Nothing about existence is stronger than the drive for immediate satisfaction.

I need some water. Grabbing the pack of instant noodles, I walk into the bathroom. There's a drinking glass next to the sink; it's not wrapped in paper. A faint lipstick stain stands out on the rim. At this point, it hardly seems worth quibbling over minor details like cleanliness. I fill the glass from the tap and wash the gunk out of my mouth and into my guts.

Next, I open the pack of noodles with my teeth and dump it into the cup. I let the water run until it's hot and then fill the cup, until the noodles and neon-yellow chicken flavoring are covered. Without a microwave, this is the best I can do. It will have to sit for a while until it's soft enough to eat.

Looking up from the sink, my reflection confronts me in the mirror. This light is not flattering. The wrinkles around my mouth and eyes have deepened since I last examined myself in the garage: impossibly dark canyons filled with spiky black hairs. I'm not so sure how much good shaving will do. I don't think I can get the head of the razor all the way to the bottom of the craters lining my face. My hair is a wild mess, still greasy despite the soaking in the rain. Grey streaks are standing out on the sides in stark contrast to my normal jet black.

I guess I've been under a bit of stress lately.

Peeling back my lips, I take a look at my teeth. They're yellow and slimy. A dentist with bad teeth—oh the irony. I take the toothbrush out of the packaging and plop a generous dollop of paste down on the bristles. Staring straight ahead, I brush until my gums start to bleed, pausing only to spit out the frothy mixture of blood and mint, reapply the toothpaste and do it again. Small circular strokes, up and down, back and forth, up and down, back and forth. The bleeding intensifies while I stare straight ahead into the mirror too focused to even blink.

In the bedroom, I hear the TV turn on and the bed springs creak. I keep brushing, up and down, back and forth, not blinking. The channels start changing, I can hear an announcer for a soccer game cut-off by a woman selling jewelry interrupted by an audience whooping.

I pause the brush running my tongue over the front of my teeth still bumpy with plaque. Again!

Up, down!

Back, forth!

The handle of the toothbrush flexes under the strain as I press down on my molars. Plaque, you will find no quarter here. The plastic strains as I excavate gunk from every crevice.

In the bedroom, the TV is still flipping channels at a manic rate. Soccer to jewelry to talk show to soccer to jewelry to talk show.

Up, down, back, forth, up, down, back, forth. The brush is a whir in my hands; cleaning teeth is what I was put on this planet to do.

Updownbackforthsoccerjewelrytalkshow.

With a loud *SNAP*, the head of the brush goes flying by my chin. The neck, now sharpened like a prison shiv, sinks deep into my tongue piercing it at the center.

I stick my tongue out at the mirror; the blue plastic handle stands firmly at attention wagging phallically back and forth. It's stuck in there pretty good.

Pressing the tip of my tongue against the back of my bottom row of teeth and grasping the handle, I yank.

Nothing.

I yank again.

Nothing.

This time I put my foot up on the sink, wrap my arm underneath the crook of my knee, lean over and grab the handle. Using my leg as additional leverage, I drive my head back and press my arm forward until the shiv loosens, then pops free. Blood sprays across the mirror and fills my mouth as I tumble backwards into the bathtub taking the shower curtain with me. I catch the edge of the tub with my ribs and feel them crack as all the air rushes out of my lungs in a *Whoomph*.

Lying in the tub with the plastic curtain wrapped around me like a condom, I try to spit the blood from my tongue towards the drain. It doesn't have the distance and instead dribbles down my chin before settling into the folds of my neck. Outside of the bathroom, I can hear the TV changing channels, oblivious to the thrashing taking place in the tub. In any case, calling for help right now is not an appealing option.

I take a deep breath to assess the damage. It hurts badly, but it appears both lungs are still capable of inflation. Wrapped in this prophylactic it's impossible to gain the necessary leverage to make it back to my feet. I scrunch my ass towards my heels and reverse-crawl my way out of the tub flopping down onto the floor of the bathroom. From this angle with my head lying on the tile, I have a perfect view of the forgotten horrors underneath the vanity: tampons, dried cockroaches and used Q-Tips.

Rolling to the left, I wriggle one arm free from the shower curtain pushing the plastic down past down my body and my feet until I'm completely free.

Lying still on the bath mat and gritting my teeth, I forcefully draw another deep breath in through my nose. Lungs expand and my eyes water as electric currents of pain from the cracked ribs shoot through my sides and straight into my brain. I cough and a thin mist of blood marks the air above my face.

Too much too soon.

I take a shallower breath and the pain drops from a ten to a six, enough for me to make it back up to my feet. The mirror confronts me again. Blood from my punctured tongue is spilling out of the corners of my mouth staining my chin and neck. The blood mist settled over my face giving the illusion of freckles. I look like a vampire in some shitty B-movie.

The TV has stopped changing channels.

My mouth tastes like metal. Leaning over the sink, I spit, then spit again and again and again. That is a lot of blood. The stew of blood and spit is thick; my eyes make lazy circles tracing its route down the drain.

Tongues heal quickly. I don't remember if I learned that in

dental school or read it on the internet. It doesn't matter; in either case, it seems reasonable enough to be true.

Cracked ribs do not heal quickly. That one just seems to be a common understanding.

A wheeze turns into a cough and the electricity is turned back on in my abdomen. This leads to more wheezing and more coughing—an endlessly painful cycle of the chicken or the egg. I take a seat on the toilet and wait for it to pass.

In the bedroom, the TV is blaring. It sounds like an infomercial. I think I need to lie down. Grabbing the dirty mug full of noodles with one hand and clasping my side with the other, I hock one more crimson loogie into the sink and head towards the bed.

Kurt lies on the left-hand side closest to the bathroom door. Three pillows prop his head up, one hand is tucked into the waist of his jeans, the other is gently cradling the remote. Mouth slightly agape, his eyes don't leave the TV as I enter the room.

I pause for a moment and then place the mug on the nightstand and gingerly settle into the bed next to him. The springs creak under my weight causing the pillows under his neck to shift. He sighs, annoyed and readjusts, eyes never leaving the screen. I stare at him for a minute as he settles back down, then turn towards the tube.

I'm lying in a cheap motel bed, penniless, unloved and broken but not alone. Life is interesting in strange ways.

Kurt picks up the remote and starts flipping through the stations again. He changes the channel so fast there is no way to process which show he just skipped over. This must be one of those superpowers only the dead possess, TV telepathy or something. The motel only has the most basic cable package. I count thirteen channels which he cycles through three times before settling on the soccer game. It looks like Telemundo; the announcer seems very excited over what I'm not sure.

My mouth fills up with blood again, forcing its way down my throat into my lungs, causing me to cough and press my injured ribs. I suck in my cheeks around my tongue and then spit a tremendous glob of DNA at the wall on my side of the bed. It makes a wet *GLOOP* sound on contact and begins sliding towards the salmon carpet. I cough again wetly, and then add a second deposit this time directly on the floor.

Kurt is pressed into the pillows seemingly mesmerized by this stupid soccer game. I try to watch it with him, but I can't follow the action. The announcers yelling in another language is giving me anxiety. Finally, I can't take it anymore and elbow him in the ribs. "Change the channel," I demand.

He looks at me and rubs the spot on his ribs where I elbowed him, then picks up the remote and starts manically cycling through the stations again. My mouth has filled up so I spit another blood loogie at the wall. This is getting annoying.

Just as I'm about to lose my patience again, Kurt settles on one of those "real-life" courtroom shows. On the screen, a TV judge is yelling at a teenage girl for stealing from her mother's purse. The girl is dressed like a hooker. Apparently, she took $50 to buy cigarettes and condoms. I think there are worse things you could spend $50 on. Considering how the girl is dressed, condoms seem like an especially prudent investment in her future. The judge disagrees and sentences her to some sort of boot camp. The mother cries but agrees and thanks the judge for her help.

"It's not easy being a single mother of a teenage girl," she laments through sobs, dabbing at her eyes with a wadded-up Kleenex.

I add more material to my crimson wall-hanging.

The girl sneers at her mother and says to the judge, "Bootcamp don't matter. I'm fourteen, I'll do what I want. You can't make me go."

A very serious-looking man wearing fatigues with pants tucked into his combat boots enters the courtroom and marches up to the girl. He stands in front of her with his feet shoulder width apart, covering her with spittle while yelling drill sergeant-y things. The girl holds out for a full fifteen seconds before her lip begins to tremble, and she starts sobbing like her mother. The camera cuts to the bailiff laughing in the corner. The judge nods with satisfaction; another job well done. This is high entertainment. Kurt seems to be enjoying it.

Blood fills my mouth. I add two more splotches on the wall in quick succession and watch them race to the floor. The noodles should be edible by now. I reach for the mug on the nightstand and take a sample. It's still crunchy but close enough.

Tilting the mug back I guzzle the noodles and start crunching away. The salty broth hits my wounded tongue and sends bolts of pain exploding through my skull. I swallow my mouthful and then take the rest of the broth from the mug and hold it in, letting my tongue bathe in the sodium. It's almost unbearable but I endure. The pain is so searing hot that it must be cauterizing the wound. Finally, I swallow the last mouthful and pant letting the wound air out a little.

Kurt is still watching the courtroom show. A man appears to be suing his ex-fiancée to get the engagement ring back. He's riveted.

I spit on the wall again and examine the results. It's tinged red, pinkish, no longer the deep crimson.

The woman pawned the ring. The judge gives them a very convincing lesson in property law; apparently possession is nine-tenths. Looks like the scorned husband is screwed. Better that he finds out now.

It's a commercial so I elbow Kurt in the ribs a second time. He flinches and rubs the spot on his side again annoyed but takes up the remote and starts flipping through the channels. Finally coming to a stop on one of the home shopping networks.

Some sad old celebrity is selling a pressure cooker with their picture on the box. The celebrity smiles through the fake tan, his wrinkles standing out even against the Botox. While maintaining forced eye contact with the camera, he spoons some pulled pork out of his contraption and onto a plate. It apparently falls right off the bone.

"This could have been you," I say turning my head towards Kurt and pointing at the screen. "I mean if you hadn't fucking killed yourself."

He doesn't acknowledge me.

"This is the final stage of celebrity. Helpless groveling, preying on the nostalgia of an adoring public, trying to squeeze out every last dollar. There is no such thing as dignity; all that matters is survival."

I stare at him, watching the reflection in his eyes as the celebrity prances around the screen. After a moment Kurt notices I'm not going away.

"It amazes me, the will of instinct," he begrudgingly concedes, clearly hoping this will be enough of an answer for me to leave him be. It isn't.

"I wonder what you would have become of you had you lived into your thirties. I mean, if you can't process your twenties without blowing your brains out, you should see what happens to you in your thirties. That's some heavy shit, man."

Kurt turns his head and looks me up and down. Some blood and Ramen noodle broth trickle down my chin. I return his gaze. My mouth hurts and today has been a real shit. In fact, this week, month, year and life have all been a shit. It's unfair but I'm annoyed and feel like taking it out on someone. I need to find someone to pick on, and I currently have only one option.

Kurt looks like a man to me—just another skinny bro. I think I'm becoming numb to his presence. I suppose if he was in his twenties today, people would identify him as a hipster of some sort, just another guy in jeans and flannel. Maybe the whole grunge thing needed to happen first.

"Do you think by now you'd be on one of these shows, all cleaned up, smiling a dead plastic smile, while pushing a TimeLife Music Best of the 1990's CD boxed set? Maybe you'd have some really stiff co-host who would rip a hole in the knee of his jeans and strap a flannel shirt around his waist and you two could playfully bounce back and forth off each other. 'Just $9.99 a month! Cancel anytime! Kurt, give 'em that number again.'" I say raising my voice up an octave, pantomiming his imaginary co-host. I almost feel bad about this, but I can't deny it's making me feel better.

On the screen, the washed-up celebrity is now chopping up carrots and dropping them into a cooker filled with broth and potatoes. A medicated audience oohs and then applauds as he brings out a second cooker filled with the finished stew. He spoons some into colorful plastic bowls and a PA starts handing them out to the audience. After his first taste, a man in khakis and a nondescript blue sweater almost falls out of his chair; the stew is *that* good. The celebrity is very impressed with himself.

This all seems very authentic. I should buy this pressure cooker. Another reminder that I don't have a credit card anymore.

The camera pans into the audience and finds a woman who had a hit single in the eighties. What a coincidence! She claims to already have one of the pressure cookers at home and raves about how easy it is to clean and how little counter space it occupies.

The audience receives another injection through their seats and nods dreamily as the director fades into a video package of the singer at home cooking chop suey for a dinner party full of comatose friends. She stares at the camera and smiles like a zombie.

The secret is the sauce is made out of people.

Kurt feels my eyes on him. "I'm not like them," he says pointing at the screen.

I decide to keep pushing to see how far I can go before he breaks all over me.

"At our most basic everyone is like them," I respond. "Self-respect is a luxury afforded only to the rich. It's a commodity you keep if you can afford to and sell if you can't. Being famous just adds leverage. It makes your dignity more valuable. People will pay to watch you fail instead of just reveling in it for free."

Kurt is doing his best to maintain his cool, but I spot a small twitch underneath his left eye. Seeing my punches land is like a pressure release in my head. I can't help but continue pressing forward.

"Seriously, you can't maintain artistic integrity and

mainstream acceptance. The two run counter to each other. Nirvana could straddle the line only because killing yourself made the band just dangerous enough to be continually relevant. If you didn't pull the trigger, at some point over the last ten years, your songs would have been used as jingles for Coke. Or you would have been collaborating with pop stars and writing songs for Michael Bay movies. Don't get me wrong, it isn't entirely your fault or even necessarily a conscious decision; we all get lamer as we get older. You either accept it or blow your brains out."

The twitch under his eye accelerates, pulling the skin around his mouth up into a sneer.

"I told you your thirties are a whole 'nother thing," I add.

I think he's finally going to break and yell at me. I need him to yell at me because at this point anger is the only emotion I can recognize. Anything else would be disingenuous, and if nothing else, we should strive for authenticity.

My mouth fills up and I spit another blood loogie at the wall. The bleeding seems to be slowing down a bit. It looks like someone was stabbed in the corner of the room.

Kurt sighs again and brings the twitching under control. Rolling his eyes, he says, "My whole existence is for your amusement and that is why I'm here with you."

Even my delusions and/or ghosts and/or imaginary friends are fucking sarcastic. If he plans on staying here and watching my cable, he should at least spring for part of the room.

The compulsion to use again is overwhelming. This is the longest period of sobriety in my adult life. All of these feelings are inconvenient. Maybe the maid left something lying around I can huff.

I turn towards the loogie side of the bed wincing as the weight shifts onto my ribs and pull open the drawers on the end table; they're empty except for a phonebook from 2007 and a Bible. The phonebook looks like it's had more use.

My back screams as I pull myself off the bed; it's tightened up after flailing around the tub. Kurt watches as I comically limp back into the bathroom with one hand gingerly on my hip like an old man.

Bending down to open the doors under the sink sends lightning shooting through my sides, enough to turn off the lights in my head for a brief second. I stagger against the rising blackness then recover. The only things under the sink are a toilet brush and can of Ajax.

There are probably enough foreign substances on that toilet brush to knock me off my feet for a week, but even at my lowest I'm not ready for that horror. The Ajax is more interesting. I scoop it up and carry it back into the bedroom. The acrid smell of the ammonia is overpowering, watering my eyes and scrunching up my nose. The back label warns to keep away from eyes and it's potentially fatal if ingested.

Sounds like someone doesn't want me to find out how much fun it is. I hold it up and shake it at Cobain.

He doesn't seem excited.

Shuffling over to the TV, I empty out about a dozen of the white flakes on top of the set. On the screen, the washed-up celebrity is showing how easy it is to clean the pressure cooker. His eyes gleam with the glassy sheen of a fresh corpse—mouth frozen in the fake smile.

I lick my pinkie, then roll it through the powder coating the tip in flakes. I gesture the finger towards Kurt as an offering and raise my eyebrows. After a mild hesitation, he shakes his head no. Disappointed, I turn my back to him and look at my finger. The chemicals haven't burned a hole through it yet. Well, no going back from here. I bring my pinkie up to my nostril and inhale sharply.

The pain is immediate and regrettable. It travels up my nose burning all the hair inside before settling directly behind my eyeball like a sword pushing outward. My head shakes back and forth like a dog with a porcupine quill in its nose.

"Whooooo! Oh shit, motherfucking, cock-fuck!" I don't know the correct combination of swears for this situation. Forgetting the pain in my back, I push away from the TV, bolt upright, and bounce around on one foot. This has to get out of my head somehow.

With eyes squeezed tight, I manage to hop into the bathroom, hit the stopper in the sink, and turn on the water. The burning has moved from behind my eyes and into my frontal lobe, setting my face on fire. I need to put it out.

I throw my face into the sink and inhale deeply through my nose. The water rushes in making my eyes feel like they're floating. I come up for a deep breath through my mouth and then plunge back into the water and exhale it through my nose pushing out the water, boogers, blood and chemical cleaner. Another deep breath and then repeat, more boogers and blood and less cleaner. I repeat the process twice more before the fire in my skull is brought down from raging inferno to smoldering embers.

The mirror shows a horror movie. Bloody, watery mucus is running down my nose around my mouth, mixing with blood and spit from my tongue and dripping off my chin.

I look back into the bedroom at the trail of destruction I left on my way to the bathroom: one shoe with a sock still inside is lying in the middle of the room, the comforter is torn off the bed, and the TV is lying on its side. I don't recall any of this explicitly but it's not surprising.

Kurt stands with his head tilted to the left still watching the sideways TV. The infomercial seems even more farcical when it's flipped ninety degrees.

I grab a towel and wipe the red snot off my face then throw it on the ground. I would have a hard time explaining to anyone who came in the room that no one was murdered in here. It looks like a crime scene. I suppose this is what you should expect when you run a motel shitty enough to not require a credit card as security for the rental. Maybe the maid will just be happy I haven't flung shit on anything. I think if it was my job to clean rooms, I'd much prefer to clean up a little blood and phlegm than to deal with poop. Although, she's also probably not getting a tip out of me. Too bad.

I spit again, this time into the sink, pinkish. The blood spurting out of my tongue has slowed to a trickle. It still stings terribly. Ramen noodles were a bad idea.

I grab some toilet paper and roll up two small wads, one for each nostril just like I've seen on TV during football and basketball games. I think I need some sleep. Tomorrow will be a day for figuring things out. I'm sure if I concentrate long enough, I can find a way out of this.

The thing about leading a charmed life is it sets your expectations, and I've heard maintaining a positive attitude is at least half the battle. It would be nice if I had a coach or some more support here for a little inspirational speech or something. I don't think Kurt ever played a sport when he was alive. I think about asking him for some words of encouragement but that was really not his thing at all. It's just me and a grunge zombie against the world.

Picking the comforter off the ground, I drape it back over the bed, then kick off my remaining shoe and sock, strip down to my underwear and crawl in. Facing the wall with Kurt still standing over the TV behind me with his head cocked sideways, I watch the blood loogies on their long inevitable march towards the floor. It's like counting sheep and accomplishes the same trick. Half-heartedly, I summon one more wad and hack it up against the wall. The blood has slowed. It doesn't really stick, and I feel myself start to doze.

At some point during the night, I register when the TV clicks off. The bed shifts as Kurt gets in behind me on the other side. Before long he's breathing deeply with warm breath on my neck. I reach back in the darkness, grab his left arm wrapping it around under my armpit and over my chest. We're spoons. He sighs slightly but doesn't protest. I finally stop feeling for a moment and melt into the black.

CHAPTER FOURTEEN

Sugar and Caffeine

LIGHT SHINES in through the cheap thin blinds, flooding my eyelids, making sleep impossible. The blinking alarm clock on the nightstand says 12:00, but I guess anything more specific is irrelevant. I sit up, yawn and exaggeratedly stretch. The room slowly comes into focus. There's a lump in the bed next to me. Magical little endorphins rush into the pleasure center of my brain. Kurt is still here. A smile tugs involuntarily but unavoidably at the corners of my mouth. I feel like the pretty girl in a romantic comedy.

The verbal bloodletting from last night combined with some real sleep has done wonders for my morning mood. I swing my feet off the bed and yawn.

As I slowly become more awake, I unfortunately become aware of the throbbing mass of jelly sitting on my neck where my head used to be. The *Kurt Cobain Loves Me* high starts wearing off. As more of my body parts check in, the less likely it is that today will be in any way less shitty than yesterday.

It feels like a cattle prod is jammed up my nose.

My mouth is full of a chalk-like substance, impossibly dry.

My lower back is tender and without a shirt on I can see an angry bruise stretching from the bottom of my back down to my ass.

The more reality settles in, the more my mood starts to fade.

I stick a pinkie into my nostril and pull out a dime-sized wad of jagged dried blood. It glows in the morning sunlight like a hideous ruby.

Grabbing a Danish from the pack, I stick my head in the sink and drink deeply from the faucet, then take a large bite out of the cheap pastry. The combination of hydration and refined sugar levels me out a bit.

Kurt is still in the bed wrapped snugly under the covers, sleeping the sleep of the dead. I take another bite of the Danish and consider him, this odd creature that has attached itself to me. His eyelids flutter delicately as he coos softly in his sleep; I don't know what he is or why he could be so fucking tired.

My mood is seesawing erratically yanking me up and down. Despite desperately needing the supervision, I can tell I'll be nothing but bad company today.

I sigh and inhale the last bite of the Danish. Little flakes of pastry and sugar dot my chest. There are many things that need to be accomplished today, my current state of affairs is unsustainable.

First, I need to get out of this room before someone sees what I've done to it. This place is no palace but I still don't need the hassle.

Second, I need to find a way into my practice to get to that cash in the storeroom safe. Money is life's greatest lubricant. The more money I have, the less problems.

"More money, more problems" is a stupid colloquialism rich people say to make themselves feel like a fighter, tricking themselves into feeling like life isn't just sitting there on a silver platter for them. Everyone thirsts for drama until they have it.

With that cash I exist again. I can get an apartment. I can hire a real lawyer. I can unlock the rest of my money. I can get back to work. The world's axels always turn more smoothly for those with the grease.

Third, I need to get my family back or at least a respectable illusion of family.

That's a big list for one day. We have a lot to do. I want to get going. I work my way around the room picking up my clothes and gathering the last of the food and money into my pack; purposely making a big production of it so Kurt will get the hint and wake up. He flips over apparently unimpressed by the noise I'm making.

Once the girls got to a certain age it became impossible to wake them up too. They transitioned from getting up at the crack of dawn to sleeping until noon somehow without crossing through a reasonable sweet spot. Nothing irritated me more than sitting around waiting for them to wake up on the weekends. If you tried to get them up, they just turned awful. Not being held captive by their hormonal imbalances was one of the good parts of living in the garage.

It's nice to remember the bad things too. Dwelling on the other side would just prey on my already tenuous will.

I can feel my mood bottoming out again. I give Kurt a "gentle" nudge to his backside, and he tumbles out of bed, dragging the sheets and pillows with him to the floor. I hit him harder than I meant to and for a second I'm shocked at my own violence, but apologizing seems like an admission of weakness.

He looks up at me between greasy blond bangs with hate boiling in his eyes, adrenaline pumping from his brain into his heart or whatever black guts are keeping him in this plain. Breathing heavily like an animal, for a second it looks like the violence is going to be reciprocated. We lock eyes like two lions crossing paths on the Sahara. Teeth and claws or nuzzling and purring? Our snuggle last night fades from memory and now I'm ready for either scenario.

"The fuck?" He turns his head breaking the tension and hack-coughs into his fist.

"We need to get going. Get your stuff together," I command. He doesn't actually have any stuff. Why would he?

I pull my dirty pants and stained, white t-shirt on as Kurt untangles himself from the cheesecloth bedding and stretches. Slipping on my shoes, I strap the pack over my shoulder, and am ready to hit the road. My first night off the grid is over. To show for it I've already got a busted-up mouth, a sore back and dwindling money wad. Another night might be enough to kill me. It's time to get plugged back into civilization.

I open the door letting fresh air flow in making it painfully obvious just how stale and stagnant our room is. Walking out into the covered porch that connects all the rooms on the second floor, the sun is shining and the sky is clear, a marked difference from the storm that drove us into this fleabag in the first place. My mood yo-yos back up with the new day sunshine and I regret knocking him out of bed. Any communication skills I once possessed have become severely compromised.

Kurt steps out behind me and closes the door. I feel like a

guy who found a stray dog and hopes it follows him home. Come on, boy. Maybe I should fill my pockets full of treats; heroin or something. I open my mouth to apologize but I can't find the courage to make the words come out, so I turn my back and start walking. He follows me anyway. Apparently, I'm not the only one with only bad options.

We make our way down the stairs and onto the shoulder of the road that runs in front of the motel. No one else in this place seems to be stirring yet. We should be able to make a clean break.

The sun is warm but low on the horizon. It feels early, maybe before 7 a.m. There is no way to be entirely sure. We slip out and onto the shoulder of the road. It will be a long walk to my office but there isn't any other choice.

Kurt shuffles quietly behind me, head down kicking at the pebbles in the gravel.

"It's going to be a long walk," I say.

He nods indifferently, head still focused on his feet.

"We have to go to my office. I have a safe there with some cash in it. We need the money. At the rate we're going what we have will only last for two or three more days at most," I explain.

Kurt doesn't look up. I've never done this on foot before, but I reckon it will take at least half a day. This march would be a lot easier with a little bit of conversation.

"Are you okay?" I ask trying to be sensitive.

He shrugs and replies, "Lack of iron and/or sleeping."

His glib response turns me sour again. I don't know why I would expect something other than whining out of him. That does seem to be the calling card for the generation he spawned. I don't have the spirit required to try and pull anything more out of him.

Seems exhausting.

We trudge along in silence. With nothing to occupy my mind, all my thoughts turn to the girls. I wonder if anyone misses me. Before long, the sun is higher in the sky and I'm covered with a thin layer of sweat.

My feet hurt from walking.

My back hurts from falling.

My tongue hurts from stabbing.

My soul hurts from sucking.

Too quickly it feels like we've been marching for days, but in reality, we have probably only made it a mile or two. I'm not entirely certain how far away the office is; I just know we aren't close yet.

Change jingles in my pocket. A gas station with a convenience store a few hundred feet off in the distance slowly comes into focus. I glance over my shoulder at Kurt. He looks like crap: skin yellow and thin enough to see the veins underneath, dark bags under his eyes. I hardly recognize him. Maybe this is what heroin addicts look like when they exercise.

I make the executive decision that a stop at the store, despite the cost, will boost morale. Also, if we get into the office, we'll be awash in cash. The days of accounting for every penny will soon be over.

A bell over the door rings as we enter. Two kids with pre-teen acne are drinking slushes and staring at the magazine rack straining through the plastic bags shielding the porn rags for a glimpse of pink areola.

We make our way past the kids to the back cooler where the full sugar energy drinks are two for $3. That seems like a good enough deal. Maybe a little sugar and caffeine will improve Kurt's look.

I pay, then Kurt and I stand outside the store drinking them down in long gulps. Some of his pallor subsides but he still looks to be on the verge of puking. I don't feel so good myself. I've made millions as a sidecar to the soft drink industry, mopping up their damage, and it's hard to understand their appeal.

My feet hurt and my lower back is becoming a problem. This sugar spike should last for a little while. I'm still preciously short on calories. I haven't seen Kurt eat anything over the past two days. What would he eat? Ectoplasm or something?

We squint through the late morning sun looking for a way out. The kids' bikes are leaning against the side of the store shimmering like the Holy Grail. I elbow Kurt in the ribs and nod towards the bikes. He grimaces from the contact and a dribble of energy drink squirts down his chin. He sees the bikes and nods in agreement. The boys are still in the store sipping on sugar water and trying to foster the courage necessary to pick up one of the magazines. No one is watching us; we're boring old white guys with boring old white guy areola.

I pull one of the bikes off the wall. It's a BMX-style rig, not made for speed or comfort. Would it kill these kids to ride something practical? I'll probably be doing him a favor by stealing it. Kurt stands with his hands in his pockets looking at the other bike, not touching it.

"Come on, let's go," I say sharply through clenched teeth.

He just stares at the bike and then at me, shaking his head. "No."

I sigh deeply. There is no time to argue. I don't really want to get busted stealing a bike from some horny kid.

"Fine. Get on the pegs, you lazy bastard."

I sit down on the seat and Kurt loads onto the pegs over the back wheel, putting his hands on my shoulders. Dust flies out from behind us as I make a mad dash for the street, slamming the pedals up and down with everything I have, knees almost reaching my chin. Kurt holds on for dear life or whatever hellish magic it is that's keeping him here.

The store fades into the distance and I slow down from the breakneck pace. We're making more reasonable time now towards my office. Kurt stands over my shoulder with the wind in his hair. He looks like a dog with its head out the window, happily oblivious to the labor required by the pedals. Color has returned to his face; it looks like he's having a grand time of it. I'm so happy.

The bike is hard work, especially carrying around 160 pounds of literal deadweight; my feet and back scream in protest but the progress is worth it. Powered by equal parts sugar, caffeine and hope, we make quick work down familiar backroads. Cars whip past at unsafe distances, as passengers crane their necks to have a look at the two bums on a bike. We're safely within the service orbit of my practice now, and no doubt some of the gawkers are people for whom I've spent years scraping sludge from teeth and bills out of wallets. Thankfully the pedals require my sole focus, and I don't have the excess energy to process exactly what any of this means on a human level.

Eventually, I lose myself in the drudgery of constant movement. Thoughts cease their relevance, and we move through the world.

CHAPTER FIFTEEN

Jason Bourne Shit

IT SEEMS LIKE two hours, I can't be sure. Time is hard to measure. Eventually I can see my building in the distance. Easing off the gas, I pull the bike into a patch of trees about a quarter mile from the office. Kurt hops off the back, looks around, sprints over to a tree, un-zips his fly releasing a steaming stream of piss over the trunk. He leans back in ecstasy and massages his kidneys.

I should stop staring.

I should always stop staring.

Another item on the list of problems I seem to have.

I stow the bike behind a tree three rows back from the road and peer out of the stand at my building. It looks empty. No cars in the parking lot, and no one coming or going. I think a tumbleweed rolls past.

Behind me there is the sound of a zipper going up and Kurt is ready to go again. Over my shoulder I motion him to follow me quickly and quietly. This is some Jason Bourne-shit.

We creep along the tree line behind a neighboring development of residential apartment buildings until we make it to the edge of the parking lot that rings my building. Looking left then right, I hunch down low and run towards the shrubs underneath the north facing window. This is how I see soldiers do it in the movies.

At any moment I expect to hear sirens with blue and red flashers. Like Smiley and Jorgensen don't have anything better to do than stake out my office. Kurt is still at the edge of the parking lot, standing with his hands in his pockets, looking up at the tops of the trees. He's bird watching or something.

Still hunched by the shrubs, I make a low whistle between my teeth. He looks down from the trees and searches the perimeter of the building until he spots me. Kurt smiles and waves pointing to a nest at the top of a fir tree. The look on his face is so foreign it takes me a moment to recognize what it is: happiness. At first I'm taken aback, then annoyed.

It's too much to have to explain to this idiot that this is Maine and there are lots of birds. How did Courtney deal with this bullshit?

Still annoyed I scan the horizon for trouble, then motion urgently for him to make his way over to me. He sighs hard enough even at a distance I can see his shoulders shrug, and starts slowly walking across the lot with the smile melting off his face. A slow-walking liability in flannel.

After what seems like an eternity, Kurt finally arrives at the shrubs. Me crouching half hidden by the shrubbery, and him standing straight up looking down with his hands in his pockets. Optically this is probably not my finest moment.

"What the fuck is wrong with you?" I demand. "Will you get down? We're trying to be discreet. In and out. Like Navy Seals."

Kurt doesn't look happy anymore. That seems to happen when people are around me long enough. His downgrade acts as a salve to my annoyance. He goes up, I go down. He goes down, I go up and on and on.

I pull on his shirt bringing him to my level and we duck walk under the windows up to the front door. I try the knob but it doesn't turn; it's locked. There is a handwritten sign in the window which says "Closed. Indefinitely." I wonder which one of them did that? It makes it seem like there was some health code violation or something. They should have been more tactful. Maybe some lie about me being on a tropical vacation.

Inching up the door, I peer into the window. All the lights are off. I linger for thirty seconds or so to be sure but I don't see movement anywhere inside. All the windows down this side and the street-facing side of the building have shades drawn sharply. Everything is buttoned up tightly.

I slide back down the door and sit on the ground. Kurt is on his hands and knees intently watching a colony of ants' scurry about. My right hand naturally falls on a baseball-sized rock. That gets us in the front door where I can disable the alarm, but it doesn't do any good against the fortress of the storeroom where the safe is. We'll need to upgrade our firepower if we want to complete this mission. I know right where to start. The internet was invented for moments like this.

Seized by the sudden fury of the first good idea I've had in months, I grab Kurt by the collar of his shirt, and we crab-walk then run back towards the bike.

CHAPTER SIXTEEN

Private Browsing

THE PUBLIC LIBRARY is eerily quiet when we walk in. I've always been impressed society can't figure out how to make sure everyone has adequate healthcare, keep kids fed or start a conversation on cleaning up drug addiction, but we can find a way to culturally impress the importance of hushed tones in libraries. To be American is to be sick and hungry but also to understand only barbarians make noise in libraries.

There is a middle-aged woman wearing glasses and appropriately school marm-y clothes at the front desk. She regards our approach with suspicion.

"Can I have a look in your bag?" she asks as we reach the desk.

"Yeah, sure. Do the computers here have internet?" I ask as I unshoulder the bag and zip it down, letting her examine the meager contents.

"See, no bombs," I say cheerily.

Telling someone you don't have a weapon never has the assuring effect you hope for. She looks me in the eye, tired yet exasperated, making sure I understand she is not charmed and pushes the bag back towards me.

"Computer lab is over there," she says dryly, pointing over my shoulder towards the back of the building. "Half-hour time limit. No pornography. Okay?"

"Okay," I agree readily.

She opens her mouth to say something then closes it. We hold awkward eye contact for a beat too long. I smile trying to reassure her that I'm one of the good scruffy, middle-aged, white men who roll into the library in the middle of the afternoon on a kid's BMX bike with a dead, drug-addicted, suicidal cultural touchstone on the back, asking dumb questions about internet access. What evil could I possibly bring upon this place of learning?

She sighs and pulls out a clipboard from beneath the desk. "Computer three is open. Half-hour time limit. We actively monitor the security cameras in that section and record the browser search history, so don't try anything." She seems used to people like me.

I nod and she hands over a pen to sign the clipboard. It occurs to me I should use a fake name but I freeze in the moment. I can feel the heat of her gaze on my neck as I pause before printing my name. I never was good under pressure. I guess I don't have anything to lose by using my real name; there is no value attached to it anymore. At this point, I'm a non-entity.

Illegibly I scribble my name on the sheet and hand the

board back to her, slyly slipping the pen into my pocket. She notices the pen but takes the clipboard anyway and hands me a scrap of paper with some random numbers and letter on it. "This is your log-in credential." It doesn't seem like Kurt's signature is a requirement for entry.

I take the paper and without another word she motions towards the circle of computer stations in the back.

Kurt and I shuffle past racks of books and the periodicals section where old men huddle around daily newspapers and dated copies of TIME until we come upon a ring of six computers, each housed in a mini cubicle and arranged in a circle. A black number three pinned to the outside cubicle walls signals our destination.

Cubicle one is occupied by a young, sweaty looking twenty-something wearing a black hoodie and stained jeans. He minimizes the browser when I walk behind him, shielding me from whatever he was looking at, then twists his neck in my direction and grins widely. Painfully chapped lips peel back revealing bright red gums spotted with black, shattered and stumpy teeth. Jet-black hair juts out at messy angles from underneath an equally dirty trucker cap. A sore the size of a dime stands out between his upper lip and left nostril. I'm instantly terrified of him and avoid eye contact. I can feel his horrible smile following me as I pass.

Cubicle two is filled by a woman in her mid-thirties, dirty blond hair hastily tied up in a bun over her head. Her chest heaves then hiccups as tears creep slowly down her cheeks. She doesn't seem to notice me as I walk behind her.

I look at Kurt, he's standing at the edge of the computer ring still staring at the kid with the bad teeth. The kid stares back unblinking holding the waxen grin on his face.

"You gotta pwoblem theya, Pops?" he asks.

Kurt stares into the kid's mouth, starts to reply, then thinks better of it. His jaw closes with a snap. After another moment, Kurt reconsiders and replies, "I can't complain," before quickly turning and walking skittishly over to me in cubicle three.

The kid with the hoodie stands up and watches him go by. I've seen that same look on hyenas in nature documentaries—crazy eyes with blood dripping from their jowls. Kurt and I scoot beneath the cubicle walls sheltered from his withering gaze.

A bulky beige computer sits on a shelf inside the cube. It has to be at least fifteen-years-old; the keyboard is battered and dirty from use. There are two heavy, thickly-framed wood chairs upholstered in worn gray fabric that looks like it used to be carpeting in a drab office somewhere. We each take one of the chairs and pull up to the screen.

Huddled inside the cubicle and cut off from the rest of the circle, I feel paranoia start to set in. I can feel the eyes of the kid in the hoodie still on us. Looking over my shoulder, I more than half expect him to be standing above us. He's not, but the feeling of vulnerability with my back to the entrance is almost overwhelming. My skin tries valiantly to crawl off my body and hide under a stack of books.

I jiggle the mouse and the dark screen on the old machine pops to life. After the prompt, I enter the code the librarian gave me. The computer takes its time to spit out a blue generic home screen with an Internet Explorer icon on it.

The hairs on the back of my neck are standing up. Panicking, I check over my left shoulder again. Hoodie still isn't there. Not being able to keep close tabs on him is quickly leading to another panic attack. It's hard to concentrate on anything except his rotting, stumpy teeth. I've seen thousands of teeth in various stages of decay and neglect, but even the worst redneck with an aversion to flossing and a Milky Way habit never came close to the nightmare typing away in cubicle one.

I open the browser and a fan starts humming beneath my legs as the CPU struggles to keep pace. Cracking my knuckles, I pull up to the keyboard, take a deep breath, and do my best to put those black teeth out of my mind.

I type in www.Google.com, private browsing mode: "Homemade explosives, household items recipe." I'm feeling lucky and begin.

The first hit is for a Molotov cocktail, but that seems more suited for rioting than providing the serious door busting power I require. The second result is for a pipe bomb which is much more promising. Text above the recipe warns: "Pipe bombs are illegal in most states and there is a high likeliness of device failure due to operator inexperience and gas build-up." Despite the author's misgivings about my skill level, it seems like a pretty straightforward build. There's no real trick to it: black powder goes into a pipe, fuse goes into powder, explosion ensues.

I flip the log-in scrap over and scribble down the recipe with the stolen pen. Kurt stands off in the distance over my shoulder. I follow his gaze, skin crawling instinctively, guts turning to slime and trying to exit forcefully out of my mouth as I find Hoodie filling the door of the cube. An artificial smile pasted painfully across his bright red lips. The woman in cubical two is still sobbing softly.

"You guys want to pawty?" Hoodie asks, speech comically slurred through his stumpy black nightmare teeth, one hand blocking an exit and the other rubbing his crotch.

Standing over us, touching an ever-expanding bulge in the front of his pants, he appears an unscalable mountain, an unconquerable obstacle of horrific sexuality. His smell is inescapable; it permeates everything: earthy on top but horribly sour underneath.

"No thanks, buddy. That's not our thing." The warble in my voice betrays my frayed nerves. I sound like a sixteen-year-old nerd asking a cheerleader to the prom. I'm not sure what "thing" I was referring to but I really don't want him to unzip his fly. Those teeth are bad enough. I don't want to see the rest of him.

"Whas's the matter? Don't wanna share ya' pwetty fwend?" he asks nodding at Kurt. "I know juuuust how pwetty boys like it." He sticks out his tongue at Kurt, runs it over his jagged teeth making a sucking sound. His stench clogs my nose but I'm too scared to gag. "Come into the baffwoom with me. I got some fwings to show you guys," he adds.

My brain furtively searches its annals looking for any experience which may provide guidance on how to handle Hoodie. First it mines relevant conversations, cross-indexing physical intimidation with potential molestation, searching for the correct response: blank.

Next it scans the violence files looking for some signal it could send to my fists or feet. It opens a memory of David Carradine from *Kung Fu* repeatedly kicking some helpless extra in the face. This seems like a promising starting point. It sends the information to my body in the form of a suggestion: *Stand, karate chop to the neck, front kick to the solar plexus, heel stomp to the face when he hits the ground.*

My body takes a minute and digests my brain's suggestion. It watches the loop of Carradine: *Interesting*.

I wait patiently as it reports back: *Unlikely to succeed. The ability to commit violence in an intentional or accurate way has been severely compromised by years of neglect resulting in questionable balance and extremely limited muscle mass. Please recalculate and send a new plan.*

Brain considers body's feedback and quickly calibrates Plan B: *If Hoodie attacks, roll into a ball with one arm covering our head, the other dedicated to holding our pants up until help arrives. Also scream as loud as possible.*

Body readily accepts Plan B as the only realistic option.

Where is that security camera the librarian was talking about? My eyes dart from the teeth, to the crotch, to a corner of the ceiling, to the teeth, the crotch, the ceiling, teeth, crotch, ceiling until I spot the camera aimed at the cubes, red light blinking. If there has ever been an ounce of ESP in my body, now would be a great time for someone at the security desk to run over here with billy clubs, assault rifles, rocket launchers, or something.

The crotch rubbing has sped up. Any faster and his filthy jeans will catch fire. The easiest way out may be throwing Kurt to this wolf. I'm vulnerable flesh and blood.

Hoodie is still lording over us, waiting for an answer, licking his nightmare teeth. My body tenses, ready to roll into a ball at the first sign of confrontation. Brain sends a new command to legs: *Stand up.*

Legs send an inquiry back: *Further explanation required.*

It's basic animal kingdom shit that in the face of a predator try to make yourself look as large as possible.

Legs consider this and to my surprise I start to rise. Sometimes I amaze myself. Proud of the fortitude I've shown, I look at Kurt and nod. He rises as well. Now standing, fully peacocked, Hoodie does not seem impressed. All of my steel has been used up just by standing; looking into his black eyes or his black mouth is a step farther than I can go. At least I'm no longer eye level with his crotch.

With my eyes down, I grab the scrap of paper with the recipe and shove it into my pocket. It's becoming clear if I intend to get out of this cubicle with at least some shred of my humanity intact I'm going to have to make physical contact with Hoodie.

In one coordinated motion, I sling the backpack over my shoulder and push through Hoodie's arm bar. I try to say, "Excuse me, we have to get going," as I exit, but the words come out so meekly I don't think they are audible.

We move out of the computer lab and down the stacks of books back to the front desk. My skin is still crawling, and my face is still full of his odor. Before we turn the corner out of sight, I look over my right shoulder back towards the circle of computers. I can see the woman sitting in cubicle two, chest hiccupping and crying. Cubicle one is empty. I back up two steps to get a better view. No sign of Hoodie; he's gone. I make eye contact with Kurt and raise my eyebrows. He shrugs.

All he ever does is shrug. Someone tries to rape us and he shrugs. My patience with Kurt evaporates again.

We make our way back to the front desk where the librarian looks me up and down searching for a sign I stole something. Her suspicion reminds me that I should have stolen something. Some DVDs, books, or maybe the mouse from the computer, anything I could scrap a couple of bucks from. It didn't occur to me in time and now it's too late, a wasted opportunity.

I avoid eye contact with the suspicious librarian and we exit out the front door. The bike is where we left it settled in the rack adjacent to the door. I don't even know where to go. I'm too shaken to think clearly. I could ask Kurt what he thinks, but I can't take him shrugging blankly at me anymore. We should put some distance between us and the library. Distance will make me feel better. It's about an hour away from getting dark. I have to save all the cash I have left in the bag to make we can get everything on the list; there's no room in the budget for something as extravagant as another motel room.

I pull the bike out of the rack and settle onto the seat. My crotch is already sore and raw after the furious ride here from the office. Sitting in the same spot makes me wince. Wherever we go for the night, it can't be far. The bike wobbles a bit as Kurt clambers on the back pegs. We're ready to go. I push off and coast down the hill. A weight is lifted off me as more distance is put between us and Hoodie.

There's a shelter and soup kitchen right down the street. My stomach rumbles in agreement at the thought of real food, even if it's the grocery store's expired donations. Going there would be risky. There's probably a reason Hoodie was hanging out at the library closest to the biggest shelter in southern Maine.

I think about his jagged, black stumpy teeth and his sour dirt stench fills my nose again. I can picture him locking me in the bathroom, rubbing his crotch and licking his lips, showing me whatever it is he thinks I should see. My appetite evaporates. I put my feet up on the front pegs as we glide silently down the hill.

CHAPTER SEVENTEEN

Free Ride

I NEVER REALLY noticed just how many homeless people there were until I started looking for them. For most of my life they blended in with the surroundings. It would be like noticing a bench or something. From time to time you might note the bench's existence but there's no reason to try and understand it on a level other than scenery. A bum is a thing you ignore until you are forced to roll your window up at an intersection.

But now, outside of the Porsche, the comings and goings of people on the outskirts are particularly interesting to me. Where do they all go at night? They can't possibly all fit inside the city's one shelter. There must be other absorption points hidden in plain sight.

Riding around on the bike, open to the world, another universe unfolds. It's dusk now and people are streaming out of their offices heading home to their families, houses and refrigerators full of food. I chew on the last Snickers bar and pedal slowly past the business people in their fancy clothes. I can't help but realize I've also become part of the background. People notice the dirty guy with the beard on the kid's bike, insofar as they are careful to avoid running into me with their cars, but no one looks me in the eyes. I'm a piece of the landscape like a tree planted on a city street. If you run into it, it'll fuck up your car. The consequences for the tree are not a relevant part of the equation. I no longer represent a human being; I represent a conversation you don't want to have with your insurance agent.

We drift away from the business district down to the tourist part of the city where all the restaurants are located. Seemingly everywhere families are headed out to dinner. Parents in this town are ubiquitous; they come in all types: young hipsters, older professionals, the blue collars, everyone has kids.

I have two.

Kurt had one.

Anonymously, we roll past the families heading out in droves to happy dinners, two epic fatherly failures. My girls are tucked into the luxurious home I bought for them, eating the food I paid for, presumably unaware, or more likely uncaring, their father exists only as a human road cone.

Kurt's daughter is likely enjoying the fruits of his discography's royalties. Processing through whatever issues a girl develops when her father takes a bite out of the business end of a shotgun. Presumably unaware her father has re-entered this earthly plain. For his part, Kurt seems uninterested in resuming the parental responsibilities he abandoned. I wonder how I seem.

Getting the money out of the office is the lowest hanging fruit towards becoming a recognizable human again. Regaining some semblance of humanity, however, requires a more nuanced set of directives I'm not entirely sure I'm prepared for.

The streetlights switch on as the daylight fades out. Kurt and I move on from the bustling downtown into Portland's exterior streets. My feet, back and crotch have all been stretched to their limits, so I keep it leisurely on the pedals.

There are people tucked into every available nook and crevice. By the highway underpass a group of three young men, barely older than teenagers, gather around on milk crates sharing a bottle and talking. Their shopping carts are filled with returnables and miscellaneous trash parked to the side. They don't look up as we slide past.

Down by the working portion of the waterfront, westward of the fancy restaurants and tourists, a large cluster of trees and underbrush are dotted with small campfires and the light from a handful of flashlights or small, battery-powered, camping lamps. When we get closer, I can pick up the beats of a classic rock station pumping out *Sweet Home Alabama*. I stop the bike, scanning the woods looking for the trail. For a second I consider navigating through the brush into the encampments. I picture emerging into the light of a campfire, the music stopping with a screech like a needle pulled across a record and then being beaten down by ten men just like Hoodie.

I pedal on, this time with a little more urgency.

We circle past the Walmart glowing like a radioactive oasis in a concrete desert. The store is still bustling with heavy foot traffic in and out. On the outskirts of the enormous parking lot are four beat up sedans with their occupants sitting on crumbling beach chairs, tending to hotdogs over a propane hibachi. They regard us vigilantly as if we are obnoxious seagulls stalking a Fourth of July barbecue, ready to take advantage of any lapse in guard to swoop in and claim a sizzling meat tube off the grill. My mouth waters at the thought of hot beef and whatever nitrates come with it.

Kurt is a statue affixed to the back of the bike maintaining a stony silence. These are your people, Kurt. Speak up. This is the generation of misery that followed your siren song towards the beach and watched in horror as you jumped ship leaving them to crash on the rocks and drown in the surf becoming shark bait. This is where you end up if you were unfortunate enough to take anything he said seriously.

I'm kind of proud of that siren analogy and open my mouth to share it then quickly close it before I can say the words. I'm still hopelessly annoyed with Kurt but I don't know what good antagonizing him would do at this point.

We slowly lap the store. In another section of the parking lot where the streetlights have been broken, two blank faces recline in the front seat of an Oldsmobile passing a phone back and forth in the dark. It could be a mother and daughter. Their belongings choke up all the room in the backseat; the windows fogged from their breath. Littered along the undercarriage, a half-drunk liter of Mountain Dew sweats alongside crumpled KFC boxes. We stop in the shadows for a minute and watch them. The girl in the passenger side says something and passes the phone back to her mother. The mother looks at it and laughs.

The thing about humans is no matter how much we protest, in the end we're social animals always looking for our clan and somewhere to belong. Even on the fringes of society there are communities everywhere. People are talking, eating, fucking and loving each other all over the place. Humanity and society are not confined to expensive homes and fancy restaurants. They spring up like weeds in a cement sidewalk refusing to be extinguished no matter how many times they get stepped on.

I used to have my own little corner of humanity. I had connections with people and we looked each other in the eyes. We said nice things to each other—shared ideas and bodily fluids. Now all those avenues are closed. My family doesn't seem to know or care that I've dropped off the earth. My employees have apparently moved on. I'm outside the outsiders. I'm a dirty blob of self-pitying white flesh.

These are not my people: these under-bridge-dwellers, Walmart-parking-lot-grillers, car-sleepers, woods-campers. I see them only on my way towards the bottom, drifting by like a flake of rotten fish food unsuitable for even the hungriest goldfish.

If my human card has to be bought, so be it. I don't have many hard-life skills, but I do know how to turn some money into more money and lots of money into a seat at the table again.

I am tired of pedaling. I haven't had enough to eat and my bottom hurts from sitting on the bike's small hard seat for so long. We need to find a safe place to hunker down for the night. I need some time to decompress and come up with a plan on how to get into my office.

Kurt squeezes my shoulder and points towards the Walmart entrance. A teenager with braces and purple hair wearing an army green Nirvana t-shirt walks out with a bag of groceries. His grip tightens uncomfortably in the soft flesh between my shoulder and neck.

"Yeah, that's right. They still sell a shit-ton of the shirts."

He looks confused.

"They still sell your albums in there too," I add.

His face crinkles in confusion and disgust, and he says, "I'd rather be dead than cool."

"Well you're both," I can't control myself any longer and I decide to pick at the scab of anger. "Somewhere in some air-less cubicle in some soul-less office, in some cold city, someone's bonus is based on how many units of *Nevermind* they move every quarter. That's how they refer to them too, units.

"Even dead you have been worth a lot of money to a lot of people. Since you killed yourself, they've found countless ways to repackage you, absorb you, then sell you as a safe and pointless rebellion against nothing. They put puppet strings on your corpse and have been making you dance for their supper for the past twenty years. Welcome to the 21st century, Mr. Cobain." I pause and let it soak in.

"Sorry, I thought you knew," I continue, "in the end none of it mattered." Picking on someone more helpless than me is a release valve, letting some of the insufferable bottled up blackness out. And in any case, it's the truth.

The light above us crackles then flickers. Kurt continues staring at the girl with the purple hair as she loads her groceries into a small yellow compact car.

A cop car crawls through the Walmart parking lot. By mistake I make eye contact with the officer. He's trolling for something. Time to get out of here. I turn back to the bike and start pedaling away. In front of me the sky lights up red and blue as he turns his flashers on and hits the siren. There's no point in running. The cruiser pulls up beside me as the window lowers.

"Good evening, Officer," I say hopefully.

"Good evening," he says agreeably enough. "What are you up to tonight?"

"We're just out for a bike ride, enjoying the weather." I cringe a little at my answer. He notices.

"Right, do you have any identification on you?"

I pull out my wallet and hand over the license. The men around the hibachi watch us with interest. The cop takes the license, compares the picture to my face and starts typing on his computer.

He frowns when he reads the results. "Mr. Peterson, I see there is a restraining order taken out against you." He eyes me up and down. "Your wife and kids wouldn't happen to be inside that Walmart, would they?"

"No sir, not that I know of."

Somewhere Smiley and Jorgensen are having a good chuckle.

"So, if I scanned the parking lot for their license plate, I wouldn't get a hit?" he asks, but it's not really a question.

"We're just out on a bike ride. I haven't seen my family since ..." I pause unsure of exactly how long it's been since I've seen them. "Since the judge issued the restraining order." That seems like the most correct answer.

He looks at me with tired suspicion and then surveys the parking lot. That would be a lot of cars to check. "Mr. Peterson, do you have an apartment or a hotel room you should be returning to?"

I'm caught flat-footed by the question. "No sir, it's such a nice night, we thought ..." What *did* we think? "We thought it would be nice to camp out." Again, I can't hide my cringe.

The cop sticks his head out the window and looks around. "You keep saying 'we,' is there someone else with you?"

I turn over my shoulder and look up at Kurt. He's standing, legs straddling the back wheel still frowning at the Walmart. After a moment he notices me looking at him.

"Here I am, silent," he says and then turns back to staring at the glowing box store. I'm not sure he could be less helpful.

"No officer, I misspoke." I concede.

"Huh, well do you have any place to go?" he asks.

I shake my head, "No."

"All right." He puts the cruiser in park and opens the door. "Please stand back from the car and keep your hands on the handlebars of the bike."

The cop steps out, walks around to the back and unlocks the trunk. "Come on, load the bike in and I'll give you a ride down to the shelter."

"I'd prefer not to. We—I was kind of hoping to just ..." no brilliance is coming to me. I feel like a little kid trying to barter with my parents for a later bedtime. "Ride around for a little bit longer." FUCK, that sucked.

"Not happening, Mr. Peterson. If you prefer, I can run all of these plates and then take you down to the station for the night where we can discuss how you got this bike and look through our database to see if anything matching this description has been reported missing. Then we'll have a look inside that backpack, too."

Before I can control it, I feel fear flash through my eyes and again I see him recognize it. My shoulders slump and I wheel the bike towards him. He lifts it into the trunk and secures the hatch down with a bungee.

"Watch your head," he warns opening the back door of the cruiser, guiding me in.

I plop down in the backseat and Kurt follows me in. One of the men around the hibachi tips a bottle towards me as the cop puts the car in gear and pulls out of the parking lot. The backseat smells like Clorox and failure.

Kurt still can't take his eyes off the glowing box. His eyes look cartoonishly large, wet and round like a pony in some Japanese anime or something. His pink-tipped bangs bounce gently as the cruiser jostles over a curb and pulls out into the road. His lips are moving; he's talking to himself quietly.

I pull my head closer to catch what he's saying. It's barely audible but I make out, "Look at what you are. It is revolting." I hear him repeat "revolting" three more times.

The thing about misery is that it's best when shared. I sit back, smile and decide to enjoy the ride.

As the Walmart fades out of sight, Kurt turns forward and stops muttering to himself. A comfortable silence settles over the three of us. Occasional calls come through his radio and the cop responds each time with indecipherable police code.

It's nice to be off the bike for a while. The trick is to think of the backseat as a taxi cab without the meter running.

After about ten minutes, it becomes apparent where we're headed. The cop pulls the car across the highway leading us back downtown towards the shelter. I suppose this is meant to be some sort of humanitarian act on his part. Get the hobo off the street and shove him under some roof, any roof, even one filled with drug addicts and the mentally ill. I guess there are places for people like me now. Beggars can't be choosers, right?

I can see him watching me through the rearview mirror, eyes glowing with manufactured warmth. He's apparently spent the silence getting pretty proud of himself for not following through with his threat to search my backpack or figure out where I got the bike from. He'll probably go home tonight and tell his wife about what a standup guy he is. Being a cop is about more than just cracking skulls; sometimes situations require a gentler touch.

Terrific.

The cruiser slows then pulls to the curb in front of the shelter. The cop turns and looks at me through the bulletproof glass that separates us. "Shelly usually works the intake for the night shift. It's a little bit late but I'm sure they can fit you in somewhere." In contrast to the Walmart parking lot, he's taken a softer tone; eyes now dripping with compassion. It looks like this fucker is so moved by his own charity he might shed a tear when we get out of the cruiser.

I used to make as much money in a month as this fool makes in a year, and now he thinks he's my dad. I'm probably older than him too. Being this pathetic is emasculating.

Under his watery gaze a panic starts rising in my gut. The need to get out of the car is becoming overwhelming. There are no handles in the back of the cruiser. I'm forced to wait for daddy to come get me.

The cop is still looking through the glass at me like an animal at the zoo. He seems to be waiting for some sort of acknowledgement from me. I suppose he expects me to be grateful, maybe I should put on the show he's waiting for and get a little misty-eyed, give him some story about how these are just the sort of little nudges I need to help pull myself out of this spiral and turn my life around.

We could hug and he could be on his way knowing he's one of the good ones. Maybe someone could take a picture of us and write a heart-warming article in the local paper or some tear-jerking post on Facebook. People could comment on it or "like" it or whatever and feel better about themselves and the world.

A vein has started throbbing in my forehead as the pressure builds back up inside me.

Kurt is looking down at his hands clasped tightly in his lap, knuckles white, shaggy dirty blond hair swaying gently, mumbling to himself again: "I'm a stain, I'm a stain, I'm a stain, I'm a stain." He's been taking this whole reincarnation thing pretty rough.

The cop is still looking at me, searching my eyes for some validation. I can feel the power shift subtly, but I'm not sure what to do. The last time I felt this way with a cop, Smiley turned it on me pretty quickly. My gratitude is now a commodity; what can I trade it for? I'm not sure he has anything of value other than to get me away from this place.

The problem is he seems to be suffering from the illusion this is doing me a favor. In his mind, he's showing compassion to a man not used to such wonderful tidings. In return, I am supposed to acknowledge my faults, thank him profusely, maybe slobber over myself a little, then he can return to his warm house full of good food, screw his wife on his soft, cushy bed, and every time a bell rings an angel gets its wings; rinse and repeat until he retires an old man slightly rounder in the middle and slightly grayer at the temples. Everyone at his retirement party banquet in the basement of the shitty hotel will agree—one of a kind with a huge heart. Tell it to his grandkids again: if only every cop was like him, there would be no war, no famine, no prejudice, no babies with cleft palates. GLORY, GLORY HALLELUJAH! NOW CRY, HOBO, CRY!

My body is shaking. I feel like a tea kettle about to whistle. His eyes lighten as he notices my hands vibrating. Here comes the money shot; the wino in the backseat is about to pop. The easy way out would be to give him what he wants. It'd be over in a minute and all it would cost is a tiny portion of my soul of which there isn't much left. I don't want to give in and waste it on him. I decide to see where the hard way takes me.

My brain formulates the perfect response. My mouth quivers in anticipation, an innocent victim of circumstance, unable to resist my brain's hideous agenda as "Fuck you, pig," flies up from my throat, past my tongue, over my teeth, into his waiting ears. I've never said that sentence out loud but it rolls off my tongue deliciously. Immediately I want more.

The cop doesn't recoil. For a beat, he just stares at me doe-eyed, the slur hanging in the air between us. My brain decides to try again.

"I said, 'Fuck. You. Pig,'" enunciating the last three words. They taste as good as the first time. Slowly pressure releases and the steel inside me starts to harden again.

His smile sours as he pulls back from the divider. Then rubs the corners of his mouth with his thumb and forefinger. "Fuck you, pig?" he repeats to himself. "Huh."

He opens the door and lumbers out, bypassing the back door, heading straight for the trunk. He takes the bike out, then his head disappears behind the back of the cruiser popping up again before circling the car and climbing back into the front seat.

"Fuck you, pig," he repeats again to himself, this time with a slight chuckle while slamming the car into gear.

The cruiser lurches into reverse with a metal shriek, gaining momentum as he slams down on the gas. After ten feet, he shifts the car back into park, shrugs with a smile on his face, and says to himself, "Some people just can't be helped."

Then he gets out of the driver's seat again and unlocks the back door. I flinch like a little kid whose father just got back from the bar. He grabs me by the collar, stretching it and dumping me onto the street. He turns away and leans deeper into the backseat to retrieve the backpack throwing it into my stomach as I lie prone on the ground.

"Shelly will find a place for you," he says, over his shoulder before retreating into the driver's seat, putting the cruiser in gear, and screeching away from the sidewalk.

When the car is out of sight, I crawl over to the bike. A couple of the spokes are broken, most of the paint has rubbed off the cross bar, and the seat has broken off but otherwise it still looks rideable. Even small victories are still victories.

Kurt stands on the sidewalk with his back to me looking at the shelter. For the first time, I become aware that a dozen people are milling around outside smoking and chatting with each other. Most of their eyes are on me. Suddenly I feel profoundly tired. With no better options, I stand up, brush myself off, pick up the bike and start wheeling it towards the shelter. There has a slight hiccup in every revolution of the tire but I'm pleased to see it still rolls. Also, the new paint job and lack of seat makes it less appealing to any of these potential thieves tracking my movement right now. There's no kickstand, so I stand it up against the building and walk inside. Kurt shuffles quietly behind me. As the door closes, there's the predictable crashing sound of the bike collapsing down the wall.

Inside, the shelter is drab. Off-white concrete walls ring a worn linoleum-tiled floor under a cheap drop ceiling. A woman with a plain face framed by glasses and stringy blond hair sits by herself at a make-shift desk. Shelly, I presume.

With a weary compassion, Shelly looks up as we walk in like someone who expects every interaction to go poorly but is going to give it the old college try anyway.

"Hi, are you looking for a bed tonight?" she asks cheerily.

"Yes." There is a bone tiredness deep inside threatening to shut me down. It's been a long day or something.

"Well, you're a little late and we have a full house tonight," she pauses searching for the right words, "but I think we can move things around and find some space for you."

She gets up from behind the desk and we follow her down the hall until it opens into a large room stuffed full of cots and roll-up mats. There is a buzzing from dozens of low-volume conversations and an acrid stale smell from so many unwashed bodies. A quick scan of the room reveals no obviously open spaces. Kurt surveys the landscape and frowns.

This is not ideal.

Shelly navigates expertly through the scrum picking her way amongst the masses like a dancer performing a routine they know by heart. We follow behind closely. Few people look up as we pass by.

Shelly motions towards a door in the far corner. "The men's room is over there. We have three showers; I keep the sign-up sheet at the front desk. Ten-minute intervals."

She keeps pushing through the crowd, leading us down the last row at the end of the room. "Well, here we go. This is the best we can do tonight," she says, pointing to a mat leaning rolled up against the corner of the wall.

She scrunches her nose. "Sorry, we tend to fill up here right before the kitchen opens for dinner at five. Hopefully we can make you a little more comfortable tomorrow night." The explanation rolls off her tongue naturally, routine. She's like an airline stewardess for the desperate, explaining how to use the seat cushion as a flotation device, why you should secure your oxygen mask before assisting others, or how it ends up your best option is to sleep on a yoga mat amid a sea of filthy humanity.

I nod and pick up the mat. Satisfied, Shelly turns, pushes past Kurt, and without a word, disappears into the scrum back towards her post at the door.

Kurt is staring out into the crowd, brow furrowed. He looks nervous. Shelly led us to an eight-foot by eight-foot square between two cots. There is an older woman wearing two coats huddled on the cot to the left. Two plastic shopping bags full of clothes are jammed underneath. She shivers deeply in her sleep and murmurs something but doesn't wake.

To the right, a man in weathered jeans and work boots sits hunched over a tattered paperback. He looks up and nods then returns to the book, not wanting to be bothered by whatever my troubles are.

I unroll the thin mat over our small piece of real estate and drop the backpack. Kurt quickly sits down, scoots his back up to the wall and pulls his knees into his chest. He looks like a scared puppy. If he pisses on the mat, we're going to have a problem.

I take a seat next to him. "Well, life's interesting, isn't it?" Another statement dressed like a question.

The man with the book looks up for a second, sees I'm not talking to him and shifts his back towards us.

The bone tiredness is working its tendrils through my body, shutting down critical functions. I shift the pack under my head as a makeshift pillow and lie on my side with my knees pulled up to my chest, leaving Kurt just enough room to sit nervously against the wall.

It's warm in here, but as I drift off I can feel Kurt shiver like the old lady in the cot next to us. Tomorrow will be a better day.

No, it will be a different day. That's the only guarantee, it'll be different. I can no longer remember the last time one day was better than the last. My bottom is deeper and darker than I would have ever believed.

That's the funny thing about life, family and dead rock stars, sometimes they all get mashed up together into a putrid stew of existence or something.

CHAPTER EIGHTEEN

That Smell

THAT SMELL, insidiously invading my dreams, black tendrils snaking in, making its existence undeniable, pulling, dragging me back up into consciousness. I open one fearful eye and lift my head up off the backpack. Kurt's gone. The neighboring cots are still asleep; the man with the book snores softly. Sitting up, I survey the landscape: dozens of hulking shapes, our huddled masses, illuminated only by the glow of streetlights seeping in through the windows, rise and fall gently.

All conversations have ceased, but the room is loud with the sounds from dozens of scratchy breaths grinding in and out of diseased lungs.

The dreams floating through this space are tangible and troubled. I can see them swirling through the headspace, ghosts of terrible memories and bad intentions; a sweaty man with red eyes brandishes a belt at a woman while her children watch. A junkie examines the veins in his arm, searching through a sea of diseased green flesh bubbling with infection, desperately tapping the crook of his elbow looking for someplace to stick the needle. I'm afraid if I stand up, one of these phantoms will notice and worm its way into my already crowded skull, eating away at the last of me, trapping me here with the living dead until it's time to join the dead dead. I can feel the heat of their longing gaze of fresh meat as I cower below their reach.

But that smell is back. Even here at floor level below the cots, it's strong, earthy and dead. I don't know how anyone could sleep through it. I've smelled that smell only once in my life and I know exactly the source. He's the whole reason I wanted to avoid coming to the shelter in the first place. Hoodie is here someplace with his black teeth.

I look around. Where the fuck is Kurt? He hasn't left my side in days. Based on the look on his face when we settled in here, I doubt he's wandering around by himself sight-seeing.

Every fiber of my body wants to stay put on the mat. It's my space, and false or not, there's a semblance of security on my little rectangle. Now is not the time for bravery. Brave people get raped by guys like Hoodie with his black breath on their necks and serpent tongue in their ears.

Yet there is a kernel buried deep within that nags away at me. I can't tell if it's motivated by curiosity or compassion but it gains traction as I sit sulking in the dark. After a moment, my arms and legs start moving almost despite themselves, crawling me along the rows of sleeping riffraff, taking caution to stay safely below their swirling nightmares. I follow my nose like a dog with the smell becoming more pungent as I navigate up the rows towards the bathroom.

Arriving at the door, I sit back on my haunches. Light is streaming out from underneath. It's currently occupied. Again, I'm faced with a moral quandary. I really don't want to go into that room. I could sit here, wait him out, forcing any confrontation on my terms, in a place where people are guaranteed to hear me scream. Or I could open the door and fall straight into hell.

Some choices only sound easy.

Maybe Kurt is inside by himself? I drop my face to the floor, turn my head sideways and strain to see in through the crack at the bottom. I could convince myself a shadow is moving inside but fear tends to do funny things to imaginations.

I sit up again and run my hands through my hair. Real life is dirty, full of hideous decisions, all of them destined to be wrong. I went to school and learned when a tooth has been compacted and needs to get pulled or whether a cavity can be filled or has to be capped, but I haven't received any training on what to do when your pet ghost is missing and likely being used as a sexual plaything by the scariest human you have ever encountered. My mind has become an intersection of two powerful rivers: one concerned only with self-preservation, the other some foreign notion of loyalty. I sit silently paralyzed in their competing currents, watching the door for a sign of life.

The light in the bathroom flickers off, then on again as the door makes the decision for me and starts opening by itself. If you wait long enough, eventually life turns you into a passenger.

Nostrils filled with the black scent of Hoodie, my hands start shaking involuntarily. I concentrate any remaining willpower on making sure I don't piss my pants. Powered by an alien intelligence the door continues its outward swing open. My mind again confirms my body's best defenses: ready to roll into a ball protecting the most important organs while screaming for help.

The door finishes its journey and there's Hoodie leaning against the sink looking down at me. His presence seems to fill the whole room. From this angle looking up at him again, he still appears grotesquely, inescapably, hopelessly, large. There's an unnaturally orange light backlighting him from a source I can't find. It seems to be coming up from the floor instead of down from the ceiling.

Hoodie looks unsurprised to find a middle-aged, white dentist kneeling in front of the bathroom door of a homeless shelter in the early morning hours. He looks me in the eyes and smiles, chapped red lips splitting in half, revealing his stumpy black teeth. It looks like his gums are bleeding. A shudder runs through my body pushing the air out of my lungs; in this state unleashing any sort of helpful scream would be impossible. Defensive strategy number one is already neutralized.

Kurt sits on the floor behind Hoodie, forearms propped on his knees, head down, dirty blond hair soaking wet dripping into an expanding puddle between his feet.

"Kurt!" It's meant as a warning shout, but without enough oxygen I swallow most of his name and it comes out sounding more like a gasp.

He doesn't look up.

Hoodie nods. His hideous smile grows wider as the bathroom light reflects maniacally off his crazy eyes.

"Yup, me and Kuwt been having ouwselwes quite tha' pawty in heya." Hearing his nasally lisp again makes my stomach turn. If it wasn't so empty, I would probably spill my insides across the floor.

"You and me gawt whots of things to talk about too," he says wagging one long dirty fingernail at me.

I shake my head vigorously. "No." I won't go in there.

"I wasn't askin' you. I was tellin' you. Now get in here," Hoodie growls.

I shake my head no again. My eyes start to burn as I hold back tears. One way or another, my body seems intent on evacuating excess moisture. Perhaps peeing my pants will be a repellent. I think I've seen something like that on a nature documentary. Either pee or tears, one or the other; I don't have the willpower to hold back both anymore.

I pee my pants just a little. If Hoodie notices, he is unimpressed. Lessons from the animal kingdom let me down again.

Kurt stays silently slumped against the wall. A wet spot marks the crotch of his jeans. It looks like we had the same idea with similar results. I should have tried tears instead.

Hoodie keeps standing in the doorway motioning me to come in. His sickly smile has been replaced by a scowl. Once again, I feel the now familiar disconnect from my mind and watch in horror from outside my body as my knees start shuffling the rest of my meat towards this rabid hyena inside the bathroom.

Hoodie grins hungrily as I make my way across the floor to his lair. The door swings closed heavily behind me. In this close proximity, his smell is thick enough to choke on. He touches my shoulder and I gag reflexively, a dry hack that drags some age-old phlegm up into my mouth. He keeps his hand on me and I adjust to it like someone becoming acclimated to icy water. His touch feels almost clinical like a doctor performing the same examination for the umpteenth time. My nerves start to settle. Maybe he's not going to gut me like a fish. Kurt is wet but seems generally okay.

"Welax," he says calmly through a forced smile, perhaps sensing the change in my demeanor. With his hand steady on my shoulder he leans over and props open the toilet seat with his foot.

"I'm heya to show you the meaning of all of this," he says, waving his hands around the room. "Kurt asked to see it so I showed it to him and now he wants me to show it to you."

This is Kurt's fault after all. Fucker.

There is an instinct in all of us that's even more powerful than survival, greed, or sex. It's horrible and morbid. It's the reason why we jump out of planes, slow down past car wrecks, or click on a link to watch a woman eat her own poop on the internet. Curiosity doesn't give two shits what's best for us and now it has me shuffling on my knees towards a toilet with a smelly, toothless, psychopath behind me. The responsibility of running my own life has become too much to bear. I want the comfort of knowing someone else is driving. I want to believe this has a meaning. The toilet whispers to me, promising to reveal the roadmap I'm incapable of finding myself.

I gaze down into the water and my reflection stares back, unblinking. I look like hell, like I belong in this ridiculous situation. I see Hoodie standing behind me; there is a resemblance in our complexions. He could be the son I never had.

His hand finds the back of my head and starts firmly pushing down. I stare into my eyes as the reflection in the toilet bowl gets closer and closer until the two meet and I break the surface. I don't have my mouth closed tight enough and some water slips in through my lips, swishing around my tongue. After a moment, Hoodie pulls me back up. I cough violently, spitting the water back into the bowl.

"Did you see it?" he asks.

I shake my head no. I'm not sure what *it* is, but I suppose I should have another look. Hoodie pushes me back into the water. I keep my eyes open looking for *it* but all I can see is white porcelain. Just as my breath is about to give out, Hoodie brings me back up. I gasp, then shake my head no again.

He waits as I catch my breath, then plunges me back into the bowl. This time I close my eyes. At first, it's just black and then images start swimming by on the periphery of my vision maddeningly out of reach. Lungs screaming, I emerge from the water and pull in oxygen in deep, ragged, chunky breaths.

This time, I don't need Hoodie's hand to guide me. I plunge my head back eager for my walk-about for the universe to unveil its mysteries to me.

Submerged in the toilet water with my eyes slammed shut, I can experience full sensory deprivation. Two bubbles tickle my skin as the last of the air escapes from my nostrils and runs up my face. My body relaxes as I wait for the blackness to part again and for life's mysteries to reveal themselves to me.

Colors start in the center then dance out toward the corners scrubbing away blackness little by little. In the center, sun is streaming blindingly in through half-drawn shades. Face down in the toilet, I squint behind closed eyelids until my pupils contract and I can see clearly again. I recognize the foyer of my old house. A bright orange cat is lounging lazily in the sun on the black welcome mat flicking its tail and lazily absorbing the UV rays. The front door opens violently and a man stumbles into the house.

Somewhere behind me a live studio audience hoots in recognition: it's Goofy Dad! The cat, sensing danger, jumps to its feet, escapes the mat and bounds up the stairs an instant before a boot whistles by its hindquarters. The audience starts whooping again, their feline bloodlust apparently matching the star of the show.

"Fucking cat," the man mutters, I mutter, as he, me, slams the door closed. The audience gasps and then laughs in appreciation of the taboo language.

Oh, Goofy Dad.

The camera pans ahead to the left passing by my favorite leather couch, pulling us through the living room into the kitchen where music is playing loudly. A woman, my woman, stands in front of two young girls, my girls, singing into a whisk and dancing along with the pop music. Pancakes are cooking on a griddle.

Ollie and Philly laugh loudly as Mary points her face to the ceiling and misses a high note by several octaves. The audience "ahhs" in appreciation of the girls' precociousness. Mary continues holding the note along with the music for three beats only opening her eyes when she notices the laughing and encouragement from the girls has stopped abruptly. The camera pans back to show Goofy Dad has entered the room. Philly hits a button on an iPod, killing the music abruptly. The kitchen is shrouded in stony silence.

The ghost audience "ooohs" in anticipation.

Goofy Dad eyes the girls and Mary, taking stock of the room. The three females avoid eye contact. Mary turns back to stir the batter. The girls twiddle with their phones, Ollie mimicking her big sister chin in hand swiping left and right. She can't help but be adorable. The crowd responds on cue, "Awww."

Goofy Dad is less impressed. He stomps through the kitchen oblivious, opens the fridge door, pulls out the carton of orange juice, and fills a large glass from the cupboard. Goofy Dad takes a big gulp, sighs loudly, but receives no acknowledgement.

Mary turns her back to the camera, picks up the cutting board then dumps the refuse from a dozen trimmed strawberries into the sink. The camera pans in over her shoulder. Sleeves rolled up she begins feeding the strawberry greens and two banana peels into the garbage disposal. One peel gets stuck on the way in and Mary reaches forward to tamp it down.

Suddenly, the machine in the sink whirs to life with a frightening buzz, the audience gasps, as Mary screams jumping back from the sink, pulling her hand out of harm's way just in time.

The camera pans back again to reveal Mean Dad with his hand on the wall switch. He calmly flips it off and the menacing whirring stops. Hunched over the sink with her sleeves still rolled up Mary pants from the sudden panicked rush of adrenaline. She opens her mouth to say something, then thinks better of it, closing her jaws with a snap.

Mean Dad surveys the wreckage: wife hunched over the sink, daughters staring at him with hate in their eyes. He chuckles to himself and downs the rest of the orange juice in one gulp, leaving the container sweating on the counter.

The camera trails tightly as Mean Dad hulks through the house out of the kitchen towards the front door. As he passes through the living room, it rotates then moves ahead and catches Friskers camped back on the welcome mat. Mean Dad lines the critter up and delivers a sharp toe to its ribs. The cat shrieks and tears up the stairs in an orange blur. The audience howls its disapproval as he pumps his fist in triumph and slips out the door. Music can be heard again pumping from the kitchen as the front door slams shut and the blackness oozes back in.

I open my eyes and find I'm now staring straight up at the ceiling on my back, lungs burning. My vision is tripled with images swimming over each other. The harsh fluorescent lights are back on. They beam down at me, burning my retinas. I shut my eyes and roll on my side just in time to avoid barfing back down my throat. Toilet water trickles from the corner of my mouth. I cough and roll onto my back.

How long was I under? I'd forgotten about that thing with the garbage disposal.

When I feel ready, I open my eyes again. The lights on the ceiling are only doubled. This is progress. Hoodie moves into my view grinning his black joy in duplicate.

I cough again and toilet water sprays out of my mouth in a fountain raining back down into my eyes. I close them again, count to five, and hope the Ghost of Passive-Aggressive Past has shuffled back to whatever coil he calls home.

When I open them, Hoodie is still standing over me, wearing his nightmare grin apparently waiting for me to say something. I open my mouth to speak but close it after a pause. I don't know what to say. I think I must be dead; it's the only way to make sense of everything. I open my mouth again and ask the only question I can think of.

"Are you God?" It's a stupid question but in the moment my mind is blank to other possibilities.

Hoodie smiles even wider considering the question. He looks impossibly evil.

"To yew, I might as well be," he says taking a small vial half full of clear liquid out of his pocket and shaking it between his thumb and forefinger.

"Mix fwee dwops with one full bowl of water, stir and BWOOF," with a hand he mimics a bomb exploding by his temple, "minds are bwown!" More cackling.

I throw up stomach bile and water violently, making Hoodie laugh even louder. He opens the door and I crawl through it. It closes behind me without another word.

On hands and knees, hair dripping wet, I make my way back towards the mat. Dreams of the forgotten still swirl just above my head, waiting for someone to make a mistake and let them in.

At the mat, I find Kurt curled up with his knees under his chin. His hair has mostly dried. He shivers in his sleep and mutters softly; I wonder what he saw. Hoodie's LSD toilet was rough on me, but it could have been worse if Mary's reflexes had been a split second slower. Fortunately, I have nothing to relive that could be as exciting as a shotgun blast splintering the roof of my mouth before liquefying my brain. Maybe Hoodie could stick Ollie and Philly's head in the toilet and help explain to them that their dad could be worse.

Kurt is still moaning in his sleep. "Come on over and do the twist. Overdo it and have a fit," he mumbles plaintively, "Beat it! Beat it! Beat it!"

I don't want to do spoons with him again. I want to spoon someone, just not him.

I crawl onto the edge of the mat below his feet and curl into a tight ball. Despite the mass of humanity expelling heated CO_2 in unison, there is a chill in the room. I wrap my arms around my legs and roll onto my side. The mat vibrates as Kurt shivers again. His fit passes to me and my body takes a turn shaking our bedding. We keep passing the shakes back and forth as our present find no comforts in our pasts.

CHAPTER NINETEEN
Oh, Todd ...

MORNING COMES QUICKLY in the shelter. The sun is barely up before the room is a buzz of activity. Staff hustle around, doing their best to cheerily herd the masses into consciousness.

I don't see Shelly anywhere. Her shift must be over. I forgot to sign up for the showers. From my seat I can see a line has already formed outside the bathrooms; four scruffy guys holding towels scratch themselves and avoid eye contact with each other. My hair smells like a toilet but it's probably too late to do anything about that today.

I sit up and stretch. A tendon pops in my shoulder making me wince. Only one night on the mat but my neck feels like it was stepped on by an elephant wearing cleats. My back is tight and my leg muscles scream from being overworked by the bike. I am a mess.

Kurt is nowhere to be seen. I feel the indentation where he slept and it's still warm. That son of a bitch better not be taking a shower. My misery requires company.

A young man with glasses and a thin beard makes his way down my aisle. He touches a woman on the shoulder three beds up, gently rousing her awake. He stops for a moment and speaks to her but I can't make out any words. She sits up and coughs violently into her hand. The young man rubs her back familiarly as she works out a wad of phlegm. When she finishes, he continues his march down the row.

Stopping in front of me, he nods to the man in the cot to my left who was reading last night, a regular.

"Hey, Tom, breakfast will be up in ten minutes or so. Coffee's hot now though," he says smiling.

Tom looks up and nods. "Thanks, Todd."

I hope he doesn't acknowledge me. I'm not exactly craving human interaction at this moment.

Todd pivots on his heel and looks down at me. "Hi, I'm Todd," he says cheerily. "I haven't seen you here before. Was this your first night?"

I nod, but even that slight up and down sloshes my brain around inside my skull. Being alive in this instance is not a pleasant experience.

Todd notices my grimace and puts a hand sympathetically on my shoulder. "Tough night?" he asks frowning dramatically. His lips are a deep crimson, skin perfect, cheeks flushed and peachy.

I look up at him incredulously. Should I explain the physical toll drinking psychedelic toilet water has on the body the morning after? With baby face cheeks glowing under a thin, manicured beard, Todd doesn't seem like the type of guy who could understand such a delicacy. He looks like a rich kid desperately running away from his parent's expectations. He's going to change the world or at least he's going to try until he's thirty. Then it's off to law school where he can trick some girl with a nose ring and a Prius into taking him seriously, as long as she takes the stud out before meeting his mom.

That's the funny thing about safety nets; they work until the first time they don't or until they're locked inside a safe inside a storeroom inside a suburban dentist's office.

Maybe if I ignore him he'll just go away. I put my face in my hands massaging my scalp with my fingertips. It feels nice. My jaw rolls back and forth making a crunching sound. He's still standing over me with his eyebrows raised, feigning concern or sensitivity or something with his stupid, young, dewy face.

"Do you need some medical attention?" Todd asks. "The clinic opens up tomorrow around 10 a.m. I can help you make an appointment if you want."

"No. Thank you," I reply. My throat is on fire making my words sound like a seal's bark.

He looks at me skeptically—another man wanting to be my hero so badly. If only I would let him.

"Well, okay. Breakfast will be up in a few minutes. If you need anything, please let me know. I'll be floating around here for the rest of the day," he says stretching for some cheeriness.

"Great. Thanks," I bark at him.

Tom leans off his cot with his elbows propped on his knees and rolls his eyes as Todd walks away.

"Kid means well enough. Hasn't quite figured out the correct tone yet," he explains. "They're all decent enough people and they run some programs that make things a touch easier. You'll get used to them. First night's always the toughest," he says forcing a smile. "I've been in and out of here for a couple of months now. Anything you need to know, give me a holler."

Somewhere along the way I've apparently become pathetic. So pathetic even the permanently homeless are offering advice.

"Which way to the coffee?" I ask wearily. My throat is still raw, but I must admit the prospect of some warm food and real coffee is awfully enticing.

Tom points down a hallway past the bathrooms. "Down there. Take your first right and go through the double doors."

I nod thanks and start packing my sparse belongings back into the bag. Something pops in my lower back when I stand up causing my knee to buckle. I catch my balance on Tom's cot barely keeping from crumbling all the way back to the floor.

Life is full of beauty and wonder.

With fireflies dancing across my vision, I go about collecting my meager belongings before dragging my worthless body down the hall towards the dining hall.

Through the double doors, just like Tom said, and another smell hits me immediately. There is real food here. My stomach responds to this revelation with an appropriate level of greed. It hadn't occurred to me just how little I've been eating lately.

There is already a decent crowd of rabble huddled around cheap folding tables, sipping watery coffee out of Styrofoam cups. I spot Kurt at a table in the corner by himself staring into a plastic cup of water. I nod as I approach his table and take a seat. He doesn't look up. He looks like how I feel—regurgitated shit.

I sit back and watch the volunteers hustle through the kitchen, scooping steaming piles of eggs and French toast into chafing dishes and stacking clean cups and plates. It quickly becomes evident there are two distinct groups working in the kitchen today; group one recognizable by their neatly parted hair, khaki shorts, running shoes and crisply branded bank t-shirts, move around spastically, obviously unfamiliar and uncomfortable in their surroundings. They appear to be here at the behest of a corporate giant struggling vainly to fulfill some cubicle monster's notion of "giving back to the community." A human resources rep is in tow with a camera around her neck, at the ready for any photo opportunity to spruce up this year's annual report.

Group two is more just a collection of individuals dressed casually and moving more methodically than group one, either aging hippy do-gooders raging against the machine in their dying light or petty criminals fulfilling some community service hours. They congregate together in the center of the kitchen, munching on French toast and watching with a mixture of bemusement and disdain as the khaki shorts stumble around.

I wonder what makes group one more uncomfortable: group two or the clientele?

At the center of the chaos of group one is one short, round man in his late fifties or early sixties, distinct only because of the grey dishwater hue of his skin. The khaki crew orbit around him, asteroids captured by his gravitational pull of his micro-management, periodically exploding out of his influence, wreaking chaos on some dishes or eggs before being pulled back in, unable to break the programmed hierarchy of middle management.

The small handful of full-time staff directs a non-trivial

amount of their energy into controlling and directing the chaos of group one. They face down a constant stream of questions while demonstrating the proper technique for dicing potatoes or unclogging the industrial dishwasher, then disperse to clean up the pieces from failed instructions by that short, fat grey-colored sun.

I get up from the table and fill a cup with coffee and resettle next to Kurt. It's weak and watery just like I thought, but the caffeine burns brightly through my system anyway, setting my nerves on fire. Kurt is still sitting morose, nursing his water. My headache has receded to the background muted both by the buzz I've got going from the caffeine and the complicated dance of humanity unfolding with the volunteers.

Kurt is really bringing me down; sharing misery has apparently become a two-way street.

One of the beautiful parts of the human condition is being able to compartmentalize the ugliest truth of ourselves, insisting we are good people who deserve happiness while ignoring all evidence to the contrary. It's the ultimate survival mechanism. Men on death row probably just feel like victims of circumstance. It would be helpful to my state of mind if this undead asshole played along. Instead, his moping is making it harder to forget Hoodie's late-night waterboarding.

"You okay?" I ask with all the forced cheer I can muster. "Want to talk about what happened in the bathroom last night?" I only ask because his experience had to have been worse than mine.

Kurt stares into the bottom of his plastic cup and shakes his head "no." After a pause, he's seen enough and pushes the cup to the side. He thinks hard for a second and replies, "I'm ashamed. Everything is my fault." He stops and thinks again. "I feel stupid and

... and," he stutters, "and contagious." His eyes are watery and black, pupils fully dilated despite the strong fluorescent lighting in the room. He looks small and sad, and for the first time, I register his strangeness. Even in a room full of poor decisions and sad stories, Kurt stands out as an alien of regret. I guess that's why as a general rule the dead don't come back. Some decisions are meant to be final.

A loud clatter rings through the room, awkwardly bringing conversations to a halt. All eyes point towards the dishwasher where one of the khaki warriors is on his knees restacking a dozen plastic plates. He doesn't look up or acknowledge the commotion he caused, but even from a distance, I can see all his blood has flowed to his cheeks.

His cubical general looks at him in disgust, then addresses his newfound audience with a shrug as if to say: "Some people are just untrainable." The room turns back to their conversations; appetite for public humiliation temporarily sated.

It has filled up quickly in here; there are at least a hundred people milling around waiting for the buffet line to open. Finally, somewhere in the kitchen the order is given, and one of the regulars from group two pulls back the glass that had been separating the uncleaned masses from their meal. They descend on the eggs, French toast and stale cereal like hungry lions on an injured gazelle. Within seconds the line is at least thirty people long. I get up to join it, leaving Kurt at the table still pouting into his water.

I take my place behind a shorter man in a black leather vest. He's wearing a bandana and has a sloppily maintained white Fu Manchu. He turns and looks at me, eyes wide but unseeing, sizing me up and down, muttering to himself before turning back towards the food.

When it's our turn, a pleasantly plump woman holding tongs in her right hand and a serving spoon in her left asks Fu Manchu, "Eggs or French toast?" She must be from group two.

In response to the woman's perfectly reasonable question, he increases the volume of his muttering. "Fucking fascists. Bunch of fu-u-u-cking fascists around here."

"I know, Gerald. You want eggs or French toast, honey?" she asks.

He looks at her bug-eyed and repeats, "Fu-u-u-u-u-u-u-u-c-cking fascists!"

The woman sighs and plops down a spoonful of scrambled eggs and two slices of French toast. Gerald looks down, thoroughly dumbfounded by their sudden presence on his plate and ceases his muttering for a moment. I pause between breaths, waiting to see if he is going to Frisbee his whole plate back into the kitchen. He hesitates for a beat and then continues pushing his tray down the line muttering again.

The woman behind the chafing dishes smiles at me and raises her eyebrows.

"I'll take the French toast, please," I add.

She plops down four pieces on my plate, smiles, then turns her attention to the woman behind me. I follow Gerald down the line and one of the Khaki Squad from group one adds a scoop of home fries to the French toast. There are gray spots standing out on some of the hunks of potato, discards from the local supermarkets, but my nose sends a more optimistic report to my brain. The smell of real food is intoxicating and my stomach makes a series of demanding groans.

I scurry back and take my seat next to Kurt. He's now face

down on the table rubbing his forehead back and forth on the edge. I shovel a spoonful of the home fries into my mouth. It's almost too much to handle. My glands are pumping out saliva faster than I can keep it down. After a second bite of potato, the corners of my mouth are covered with shiny spit and flecks of potato.

"You should go get some of this," I say to Kurt, trying to be helpful. "It's great."

He doesn't respond.

"We've got a lot to do today," I say between bites of French toast, "You're going to need the energy." I sound like his mom.

Kurt lifts his head and rolls his eyes at me, completing the parental dynamic. There are deep indentations on his forehead from where it was rolling across the table.

"Suit yourself," I say through a mouthful of food, "You aren't going to ruin my day. Big plans." My mood is improving at the same rate as the calories converting to energy in my gut, but it doesn't seem to be translating with my companion.

"So Hoodie showed you some shit inside his toilet. He showed me some shit too." I look at Kurt out of the corner of my eye and continue. "He showed me truths I didn't want to see, but I saw them and now they're back running loose inside my head too."

He keeps his head down on the table.

"And all we can do is capture them and shove them back into the holes we dug for them the first time. It doesn't make you a bad person." I pause considering that thought for a minute. It hangs in the air between us until I amend, "It doesn't make you *worse* than anybody else."

Kurt resumes rolling his head back and forth across the table. I am not being helpful.

I let the silence build back up between us like a fortress and he stops racking his forehead. The remaining French toast has cooled and acquired an unappealing gluey texture. I pick at what's left of the potatoes, working around the grey spots.

I notice Gerald is standing in the middle of the row of tables still holding a tray full of untouched food. The traffic in the room parts around him like a rock in a river. A young woman with long dark hair gets too close as she makes her way to the front to bus her tray. Gerald mistakes her for a fascist and starts in animatedly. Hate burns brightly in his eyes as he barks at her. The woman keeps her head down and tries to slide by. He turns and chases her retreat with a trail of obscenities but doesn't follow and becomes distracted when another victim wanders too close. The pattern repeats itself. It's like watching the Discovery Channel or something.

"See Gerald over there?" I ask nodding my head in his direction. "That's what happens when you listen to your thoughts."

Kurt looks up just as Gerald begins covering an old man with spittle, accusing him of molesting kids, dogs and his mother. Being mistaken for a motherfucker finally taps the nerve Gerald has been looking for, and the old man wheels around to confront him. Gerald's beady eyes glow at the prospect of a good fight. The din in the room quiets down again as people turn to watch these two gladiators square off in the Coliseum.

Todd appears out of nowhere, parting the crowd, lunging between the two men. Gerald is already in motion, screaming sweet truth and swinging his tray full of food towards his adversary. Before he can get his hands up to protect himself, Todd absorbs the swinging tray directly in the gut. The whole room watches as the plate full of eggs hang in the air for what seems like an eternity, waiting for the chance to fulfill their destiny. Even Gerald pauses his assault long enough to admire as the eggs splat on Todd's face tangling in his young wispy beard.

Rage flashes through Todd's eyes, and with a trembling hand he wipes the breakfast sludge off his face. Gerald recognizes the expression. The violence building like a storm in front of him is strong enough to momentarily pierce the veil of crazy; he is frozen in place watching the punch hurtling through the space between them. Then in the instant before Todd's fist finds sweet fleshy pay dirt, it stops abruptly retreating backward. Gerald looks first confused and then disappointed as one of the kitchen supervisors intercepts Todd's punch at the elbow and guides him away from the skirmish.

Another staff member joins the supervisor on Todd's other arm, struggling to control him as he thrashes with egg dripping off his chin. They drag him out of the dining room as he screams with primal force in a language that must have died out with the cavemen.

Gerald and his original target are face to face again. Before Gerald can recover, the old man turns away, scurrying over to the dishwashing station where he quietly buses his tray and leaves.

I grin at Kurt, point thoroughly proved. "See?" I say. "We're all animals just inches away from our most basic instincts."

I think I've had enough of this breakfast. I clear my tray, thanking the poor sap working the dishwasher buried under an avalanche of dirty plates and half-eaten food. He looks miserable.

We make our way through the building back outside to the bike, finding it still lying on the ground in front of the entrance. I was right last night; it's so busted up it wasn't even worth anyone's effort to steal. Pulling it off the ground; the seat is lying next to the curb. With some effort, I manage to jam it back into its post. My crotch settles uncomfortably onto the now familiar slot. After a moment's hesitation, I feel Kurt's hand grip my shoulder, and the bike leans to the left, then settles to the center as he climbs on the back-tire pegs. The tension from his touch runs through my body, a jumper cable wired directly to my heart, and it skips a beat. Kurt is being pushed over the edge again and it's spilling out of his every pore. My skin crawls underneath his fingers.

"Get over it, Kurt," I say over my shoulder. "With the rest of this money, we're going to supply up and move on." I pat the backpack confidently. "I'm not coming back here ever again."

The nervous electricity connecting us ebbs for a moment before roaring back into my circuitry. I shift the weight of his grip from my neck onto the strap of the backpack. The extra layer of cushion helps, muting his psychotic energy from a swarming buzz to a low hum.

With feet on the pedals, I begin the push up the hill away from the shelter. The bike limps over the handful of broken spokes. After a couple of hundred feet, I become used to the jagged ride. For his part, Kurt seems not to notice.

We stop at a red light at the top of the hill, and I pull the crumpled list of ingredients out of my pocket. Half of them should be at my friendly big box hardware store. There are no mysteries left in life anymore. The internet is such a lovely invention. If I was going to be careful about covering my tracks, I would source this list from a dozen different places, but I don't have the patience to shop around on a busted-up kid's bike with this electric eel of guilt shaking on my shoulder.

With no cars coming, I push away from the intersection, finding the pedals as the bike gains speed. Traffic quickly moves around us, drivers engrossed in their own mundanity, unaware of our secret plans.

Goosebumps break out on my arms.

CHAPTER TWENTY

Swiping Left

DARK PATCHES of sweat are sticking out on my shirt from underneath the backpack and along my ass from the bike seat. The trip to the hardware store was long and taxing, especially pulling Kurt around.

When we left the shelter, the sun was rising and the weather was warmly pleasant. As it rose, the heat of the day became suffocating. It is one of those days of extremes that happen in Maine in the summer. No breeze kicked up and the air has become still and stagnant; it has the tangible feeling of swimming through mashed potatoes, making every breath labored.

Heavy with supplies, the backpack clinks each time I pump the bike's pedals. Getting the first half of the ingredients was easy. Hell, some kid working at Home Depot even drilled the hole I need to run the fuse out of the pipe. He said it sounded "cool."

All that's needed now is the powdered violence, something to create the chaos. For the last few years, I've driven by Frank's Fireworks Emporium every day on my way to work. I only ever bothered to consider it when cursing the rednecks a few streets away who insisted on celebrating the Fourth of July every night straight through August. My legs keep pumping robotically, pushing the bike through the thick air as visions of explosions across the night sky play inside my skull.

The hundred and fifty foot red, white and blue bottle rocket that teeters above Frank's roof rises above the horizon; heat waves bounce off the black tar creating a magic shimmer over the emporium. Traffic on the road is sporadic.

A minivan cruises by cutting dangerously close to us on the shoulder. I pull the bike into the suction left in its wake and give my legs a momentary break. There's a slight relief from the heat just in having the air disturbed. The bike crests over the incline and we coast the rest of the way into the store's empty parking lot.

I lean the bike against the building and we step inside. It's not what I expected. Brightly lit overhead with white walls and floors. Stepping in from the sun outside it takes my eyes a minute to adjust. Thousands upon thousands of intensely-colored fireworks are stacked neatly along cheap racks that separate the store into rows. I count seven rows before I stop caring and give up. The frigid AC freezes my sweat sending a shiver down my back. Overwhelmed, I override my internal command systems and force my legs to pilot my frame deeper into the store and down the middle aisle.

My head swims with choices. I'm surrounded by red, white, blue and neon packaging shouting names at me like: America,

FUCK YEAH!, Osama Bin Explodin', The Great Bangbino, Let's Get Bombed!, and on and on. Where are these made? Is there really a marketing department that sits around a conference table sketching out names that sound like patriotic pornos? It's a cornucopia of 'broisms.

I walk through the aisle towards the back rack where a dozen of the biggest rockets are on display. A black sign with white lettering stating, "Category Four" ringed by skull and crossbones hangs over them ominously. I pick up a black tube as big as my arm covered in yellow stars, turn it over and read the label. It's just a list of chemicals and numbers that don't mean anything to me. I don't know what I should be looking for. They're selling it for $75. I wonder if we could fit it down Kurt's pants and smuggle it out of here.

Holding the tube up to my ear, I shake it vigorously. This attracts the attention of a short bald man in a blue polo who scurries over.

"Can I help you, sir?" he asks with a nasally whine, pulling the rocket gingerly out of my hands before placing it delicately back on the display.

"Just looking around," I reply. I'm not exactly sure how to phrase what I really want.

"Right, well, this wall has some serious firepower on it. These things are not meant to be fooled around with. They aren't toys," he says, scolding. "These are really meant more for the professional. The basic weekend warrior backyard fare is kept in the front of the store." He points back towards the way I came in.

I pause for a second searching for the right words. "I'm just looking for whatever will make the biggest bang for the least amount of money."

He squints at me through thick-rimmed glasses, crumpling his nose while considering what I said. "So are you looking for something big to end your sequence with? What's your lead up? You got peonies, beehives, girandoles, or what?" There is a glint in his eye now.

"Uhh yeah, we've got some bottle rockets or something, then one of those beehives or whatever. I just want something that will make a really big pop at the end, on a budget."

"How much is this budget?" he asks.

I open the backpack and pull out a crumpled $10 bill, two $1 bills and some change: $12.70 in all.

He examines the money, interest waning and motions for me to follow him. He leads us along the back wall towards a bin in the far corner. "This is where we store all of the expired inventory. Everything in there is five bucks. No returns and we don't make any guarantees they'll work." With that, he turns on his heel and heads back towards the counter.

Kurt picks up a package of bottle rockets, turning it over and over in his hands. There's a picture of a soldier dressed in camouflage pointing a gun outward so Kurt is looking down the barrel. "Use once and destroy," he reads.

I dig both hands deep into the bin and search for the biggest rockets, something at least as big as the pipe I bought. At the bottom, I grab one with fins and a nosecone. There is some Chinese lettering on it. I can't read the content list but it feels heavy. I glance at the cashier who is face down in a phone, swiping furiously with his left thumb. I pull Kurt between us and stuff a pack of smaller rockets into the band of his underwear. Kurt just stands in front of me, eyes glazed and doesn't protest.

"Be cool," I hiss at him while pulling his shirt down over the package. The bulge is hardly noticeable.

We walk up to the cashier and wait for him to acknowledge us while his thumbs work right to left across his screen. He scrolls through his phone three more times, laughing to himself. I place the rocket on the counter as he looks up.

"That it?" he asks.

"That's it," I confirm, smoothing out the $10 bill and placing it next to the Chinese bomb.

He takes the cash off the counter and fiddles with the register. "Usually the only takers we get for the discount bin are kids looking to blow up their hamsters. That thing you bought will take a serious chunk out of any rodent dumb enough to have crossed you," he says earnestly, turning back to me with four crisp $1 bills and some change.

"Great," I reply, taking Kurt by the elbow and leading him towards the door. "I know a cat who's had it coming." Kurt follows me without any protest. The cashier watches us leave then buries his face back into his phone and resumes swiping left.

Outside again the heat hits me like a wave and the sweating immediately resumes. I pick the bike up and wheel it to the side of the building away from the windows. Out of sight of the cashier, I pull up Kurt's shirt, take the pack of bottle rockets out of his pants and gently wrap the package with the larger explosive in a dirty t-shirt before gingerly placing them in the backpack with the rest of the supplies. I sling the pack over my shoulder and it rattles ominously. If this thing isn't dead, I don't want it shooting me to the moon the next time I go over a bump. I peel the pack off my shoulders and hand it to Kurt.

"Here put this on," I command, pushing it into his hands. Let him pull his own weight around here for a while. Kurt looks at me understanding. He twitches twice, spasmodically, then sadly accepts the bag and puts it on. I turn back forward and steady the bike as he climbs on the back pegs.

The road is deserted again. It feels like the temperature climbed another one hundred degrees while we were in the Emporium. It's approaching the stage where the tires could start melting to the blacktop. I navigate the bike onto the shoulder and start making the trek back up the hill towards the future.

CHAPTER TWENTY-ONE

That Winning Feeling

I'VE LOST TRACK of time. My brain is boiling in its own juices. The sun is setting but it's still body-melting hot. The heat strangles and kills all coherent thought. I am starting to recognize the streets again as they pass by. We're getting close. Traffic has picked up as people hustle home to their loved ones for the night. I can see faces through the glare of windshields. This is a small town. I recognize about every fifth one, but no one seems to notice the maniac and the ghost furiously pushing a busted-up kids' bike through the sweltering summer air.

Perhaps it's on purpose. I don't like being part of the scenery.

The sun falls below the tree line as we come to the same tree stand where I stored the bike the last time. Streetlights start to flicker on as I ease off the pedals and guide the beat-up bike into the woods, dropping it on the ground with disdain. The tires look almost bald and another spoke has broken, but in general it still appears rideable, barely. I hope I never spend another mile hunched and sweating over its adolescent handlebars.

I motion towards Kurt and he passes over the pack. I open it, spreading the contents on the ground, gingerly placing the Chinese rocket and package of bottle rockets on a bed of brown pine needles. Kurt steps back as if to disavow himself of this process and stuffs his shaking hands into the pockets of his jeans. He is degrading quickly. Face down, my lip curls into an uncontrollable sneer that I don't let him see. A distraction is the last thing I need so close to the finish line.

Taking the shiny aluminum pipe out of the bag, I untwist one end cap and put it aside. Next, I pick up the larger rocket with two hands. It's made from cardboard with red plastic fins and nose cone. A long black fuse feeds out of the bottom of the tube and is taped between the fins. I hold the rocket up and poke around at the base looking for the seam.

At the store, it hadn't occurred to me that some sharp object would be helpful for this surgery. I haven't trimmed my fingernails in weeks, so I press my thumb into the seam hunting for a hint of traction. I press harder and the rocket falls out of my hands, bouncing off a root before settling on the needles. Kurt jumps back, jittery, and braces for the disaster that doesn't happen. I pick up the rocket and mockingly feign tossing it to him. He winces then turns his back to me and walks deeper into the protection of the trees, talking quietly to himself.

I need a new plan of attack. The decal peels easily off the outside but there is no obvious entry hatch underneath in the plain cardboard. Grasping the nose cone between my thumb and forefinger, I start rocking it back and forth until the glue gives way and it falls into my hand. Underneath is more seamless cardboard. Without any better options, I put the tip in my mouth, bite down hard with my molars and pull with both hands. Something starts to rip. I hope it's the packaging and not my teeth.

My head whips back crunching my neck, sending me stumbling backward as the top of the rocket finally gives way. Stars dance across my vision as my mouth fills with something chalky and metallic tasting: gunpowder, I presume. The powder rides the air down my throat into my lungs, coating everything it passes, absorbing all moisture.

Carefully so as not to waste any more of the juice I place the rocket on the ground next to the tube before gagging violently. My tongue flails around like a dog trying to get peanut butter off the roof of its mouth and I wretch again.

It's so dry.

In a panic, I stick two fingers down my throat trying to claw the dust out.

Kurt comes out from behind the trees to watch the spectacle. With his arms crossed, he smiles slightly, still talking to himself while I run back and forth in front of him, trying desperately to bring moisture to a desert. Mercifully, one of my fingers finds a soft spot in my trachea and initiates the gag reflex, flooding my mouth with stomach acid and liquefied French toast. I let it flow out of me in dark black waves until I'm empty again and then fall back on the pine needles, staring up at the trees, panting.

Kurt chuckles and asks, "Choking on the ashes of your enemies?" When he hears the words pass by his lips, he frowns again and toes at some dead leaves lying in a pile on the ground.

Sitting up, I spot a small puddle of standing water underneath one of the bigger trees and drop to my knees in front of it for a closer look. There are some dead bugs, a bloated worm and a pile of leaves floating around. I don't see any obvious animal shit. Once again, as I scoop the water into my palms and funnel it into my mouth, I am reminded that it is merely circumstance which separates the world into beggars and choosers. I turn my back so Kurt can't see. I've already been charitable enough with my dignity for today.

It takes two slurps of the vile water to wash the powder out of my mouth, returning the necessary moisture balance. I turn around and Kurt is still standing there, watching me with his arms crossed. Without making eye contact, I go back over to where I laid the supplies and pick up the rocket holding it cautiously away from my face.

I pull up the collar of my grimy white shirt covering my nose and mouth, then squint into the tube. It's three-quarters filled with a fine black powder. This thing looks like pure bomb. Delicately, I create a small crease in the cardboard and carefully pour its contents into the open end of the pipe until it is about half full, taking special care to keep the fuse hole covered with my thumb.

Next, I tear open the package of small bottle rockets Kurt jockeyed out of the fireworks emporium. There's six of them stacked neatly together. They aren't made quite as rugged as the Chinese Rocket, so it's easy to pull their tops off and dump the comparatively meager contents into the pipe.

I fish through the bag until I find the handful of nuts and bolts, which according to the recipe, get packed into the tube above the powder. I screw the cap back onto the open side. It's starting to look like the pictures I found online. This is encouraging. Next, I take the Chinese Rocket back up and carefully extract the fuse. It pulls easily out of the fuselage and I feed it into the hole the kid at Home Depot drilled. I wind black electrical tape around the fuse and hole.

Setting the pipe bomb on the ground, I stand back to admire my handy work. Kurt cranes his neck around a tree to look at it but doesn't get any closer.

"Pretty good," I say raising my eyebrows at him. "This thing'll blow the door right off the hinges."

Kurt looks at me skeptically, blinking erratically.

Non-believer. I don't need his negativity right now. I'm going to break through the front door, disable the alarm, blow the hinges off the door to the stockroom, crack open that safe and then take a cab to a nice steak dinner, alone. My mouth waters at the thought.

The darkness of the night has fully descended on our thicket of trees. Yellow light from the streetlamp falls on us between the leaves. I still don't have any concept of what time it really is, but it seems like a good idea to wait a little longer before we start playing cat burglar.

Contrary to my old life, time is the only luxury I can still afford. With no schedule to keep or people to interact with, the traditional rhythm of a day is completely irrelevant. I could lie in this thicket for years. I bet Rip Van Winkle was a shitty husband and father too.

I lie down next to the bomb with my hands behind my head and watch the neon light stream in. It's silent. The patch of wilderness we're in isn't big enough to support any real wildlife. The only sound is the electric buzzing from the lights. Taking a deep breath, I exhale the last of the blackness from my lungs in a little cloud.

The money feels close. It's intoxicating. Since Mary kicked me out of the garage, I've been forced to feel every sharp edge of the world ripping at my flesh. It's been like tumbling down a well, bouncing off the sides as I plummet into the dark. Lying here under the trees and streetlights, I've finally settled at the bottom and it's time to start taking the fucking elevator back up. Who knows? Maybe there'll even be a little lost vial of morphine waiting for me with the money. My face can't help but crack into a smile at the thought of such a luxury.

I crane my neck to look up at Kurt. He's slumped in front of a tree with his hands on his knees, looking towards the sky. Maybe morphine will knock him out of the picture. At that thought, my smile turns into a grin stretching wider until I lose control and start laughing. It builds and builds like an avalanche rolling down a mountain. I can't control it. I don't want to.

Pine needles coat my face as I roll over gasping for air between gut-wrenching seizures of joy. It's starting to hurt my sensitive ribs, but I don't care; it would hurt worse trying to keep it bottled up inside. I'd almost forgotten what it feels like to win.

CHAPTER TWENTY-TWO

Thank You for that Information

SOMETHING IS RUSTLING the leaves around me. My eyes fly open but struggle to acclimate to the dim light. As they refocus, a small grey mole scurries by my hand, following its nose away from me. My brain starts shaking the sleep away, and I sit up to look around. Kurt is nowhere to be found. That's fine, preferable actually, I don't really need him anymore anyway.

The backpack and the bike are where I left them, but the pipe bomb has disappeared. That's a serious problem. On my hands and knees, I start frantically sweeping through the needles and crunchy leaves looking for it. There is no trace, only the discarded husks of dismantled fireworks.

How long was I asleep for? It must be Kurt. That numb fuck. I've been watching him break down, but why would he choose right now do this to me?

The anger and the adrenaline feed each other symbiotically until I'm on my feet panting with rage. My mind races as I try to focus and think about what to do next. Visions of cabs, huge steaks and morphine-aided sleep start to fade, replaced by violent dreams of squeezing my thumbs into Kurt's eyes until they pop out of his ears and splatter on a wall.

I look up at the night sky trying to steady my mind and figure out what to do next. The mole has moved on and the tree stand is still, silent with no footsteps or sign of movement. How are you supposed to track a ghost? I don't have enough money to build another way into the stockroom. The adrenaline subsides turning the anger from rage to anguish. My knees shake and I fall backward on my butt. Hopeless tears engorged by self-pity roll roundly down my stubbly cheeks.

All of the sudden, the silence of the night is shattered by the jangling sound of breaking glass. I shoot straight up and peer around the trees towards my practice, counting backward from ten, hoping this isn't exactly what it seems to be. I get to three before a familiar alarm starts ringing out confirming the worst-case scenario.

Bastard! He's going to fuck this whole thing straight to hell.

My legs react before my brain can start handing out commands and I'm off ambling through the rest of the trees towards my building. This is a time for speed not stealth. I need to get inside and turn off that alarm before all is lost and that fool brings every cop in Maine crashing down on us. The adrenaline is now fueling pure panic, moving my legs in ways I never thought they were capable of.

Despite the car crash, miles of biking, busted ribs and

punctured tongue, I manage to sprint across the grass like a blur through the parking lot to the building's front door. It's hanging wide open. A fist-sized rock surrounded by broken glass is sitting in the entry. I step over it and dash over to the alarm panel. It seems like the alarm has been ringing for hours. All the neighbors' windows are still dark but there is no chance this blaring hasn't woken them up.

It's only a matter of time before this is all up in smoke. I can't wait to get my hands on that tattered jeans, flannel shirt wearing, blue-eyed, baby-faced, antiestablishment motherfucker. There will be no easy way out for him again.

The reception area in my office looks like a war zone. There is shattered glass and paper everywhere. The alarm drones on drowning out all thought.

A better person would set the alarm code to their wedding anniversary or one of their kid's birthdays, but thankfully I was honest enough with myself to know remembering any of those when I really needed to would be hopeless. I punch my birthday into the pad killing the sound mid-bleet and wheel around looking for Kurt.

There is no time to properly break into the storeroom now. I need to retrieve the pipe bomb so he doesn't waste it and disappear into the night.

As I head towards the back of the office, the phone at the front desk starts ringing. I scramble across the mess, knocking over a coat rack to answer it. A flop sweat has broken out across my armpits and neck. One long drop makes its way slowly rolling down between my ass cheeks.

"Hello?" I ask harried into the receiver.

"Good evening. This is ADT calling to confirm the alarm has been canceled," replies a soothing female voice.

"Yup, no problems. I tripped it by accident when I was locking up." I crane my neck, trying to look around the corner. I can't see or hear anything. Where the fuck is Kurt? What is he doing with my bomb?

"Okay, sir, I appreciate that information. With whom am I speaking?" it sounds like she's reading off a script, half paying attention.

"I am Joel Peterson. This is my account." Trying to swallow back the panic rising in my voice, my eyes dart around the office looking for clues.

"Okay, Mr. Peterson, thank you very much for that information. Can you please confirm your social security number for me?" Her robotically calm voice only increases my anxiety. I can picture her sitting in an artificially lit cube somewhere, wearing a headset, while casually browsing through her phone unaware of the urgency she has dialed in to.

"035-45-2402," I reply hurriedly.

"Thank you very much for that information." She pauses. I can hear her typing. My stomach is doing summersaults. The wait is excruciating. "Okay, Mr. Peterson, that verifies. Now I see from your account you are two months past due on your bill. You are a valued customer and ..."

I slam the phone back into the cradle. Somewhere in the distance a police or ambulance siren is whining. I can't tell if it's headed this way or not, but in either case it's too late to worry about now.

In a sprint, I make it around the bend in the hallway in three steps. I almost run headfirst into Kurt. He's on his knees in front of the storeroom door with the bomb in one hand and a lighter in the other. He pauses his work for a second, unsurprised by my presence.

"Take your time, hurry up. The choice is yours, don't be late," he says touching the lighter down on the end of the fuse. The flame sparks once and then quickly begins eating its way up the line. Kurt drops it at the base of the door and backs away to watch.

The pipe bounces off the floor and rolls towards me with smoke puffing out of the fuse. After a moment of hesitation my knees unlock, and I fumble forwards sweeping it off the ground in one awkward motion.

I need to cut off the flame before it reaches the powder. Using my thumb and forefinger I grab the unburned portion of the fuse and start sawing at it with my thumbnail. It's thicker than it looks. Sweat drenches my face as the little flame continues undeterred down its path. My nail isn't sharp enough.

The sweat pouring off my forehead gives me an idea and I spit at the fuse just in front of the little spark. It doesn't hesitate traveling over and by the wet part.

Maybe I can dislodge the damn thing from the pipe. I pull at the base, but the electrical tape is wound too tightly and layered on too thickly and my fingers are too slick from sweat. Undoing it will take too much time.

What the fuck? Why is the construction of a pipe bomb the one thing in life I don't fuck up?

I look around desperately, unconsciously hopping back and forth between my left and right foot. Kurt watches intently from around the corner with his hands over his ears, waiting for the bang.

The flame is centimeters away. I need to put this thing

down, give it up as a lost cause. I look at Kurt's dumb eyes peering at me from behind the wall.

"Why?" I yell, conceding the fight, opening my fist, letting the bomb fall towards the floor.

A flash of fire lights up the air in front of me like a zipper opening in space. For a brief second, I think I can step into it and leave this plain for someplace better. Before I can complete the thought, there is a loud pop, zipping the rip back up, as I fall backward away from the explosion.

Then it's over.

I sit back up on my elbows and survey the office. A mist hangs heavy in the air, dark red, beautiful. I open my mouth and collect the suspended particles on my tongue. They taste metallic, elemental. Like a little kid celebrating the first snow of winter, I stick my tongue out again and bring in more droplets, it's refreshing.

I raise my left hand to examine what's left. My pointer finger is set at a ninety-degree angle towards my thumb. The other three fingers have disappeared and been replaced by nubby stumps pumping blood down my wrist at an impossible rate.

I've always wondered what this would feel like—the outer fringes of the human experience. It feels like the rest of life, like nothing. I feel nothing.

I hold up my hand in amazement and show it to Kurt. He steps out from behind the wall. His face is painted deep red, blond hair streaked and matted from the mist. He reminds me of an Indian Chief from some old movie.

"It doesn't even hurt," I say dreamily, pushing my mangled hand towards him.

Kurt takes another step forward to get a better look at my

hand. He shakes his twitchy, red-painted face disapprovingly. I don't know why he should be bothered. It's not his hand. I'm fine.

The bomb is gone, wasted, and now we need to concentrate on getting out of here. I stand up and move towards him. After two steps, I stumble but catch the wall with my good hand and avoid going all the way back down to the floor.

My head is swimming. It's hard to concentrate. Steadying myself, I can hear the blood from my hand steadily drip, drip, dripping on the tile floor. The walls start moving in, closing on me like a coffin. I lose full control of my knees as the ground comes up to break my fall.

Lying on my back, blackness swirls in front of my eyes and then blood and then blond hair and then flannel and then blackness.

CHAPTER TWENTY-THREE

He Tried, or Something

IT'S SORT OF gummy. When I push against the blackness, it pushes back, filling in the voids around my fingers, pressing against the rest of my body, trapping me in its simple beauty. I wonder if I can swim through it; breaststroke is the best stroke.

I pull my knees to my chest and then push them straight back until it feels like I'm horizontal. No light penetrates and I can't see through, but I have the sensation of floating.

Heaven is a jello-mold, hello-mold.

I stretch my legs until my knees and hips crack. I push my arms out over my head and the tension in my shoulders evaporates immediately. I can't hear anything or see anyone.

I want to stay in my little black jello-mold forever, mellow-cold.

I let my eyes close and relax, filling my lungs with the perfectly warm air from inside my cocoon. I think it's time for another nap. I pull some of the blackness towards me and lump it in thicker around my neck like one of those travel pillows people use on planes. It's perfect. My back relaxes, my breathing slows, and I start drifting off again into the silence.

If this is my eternal slumber, it's well earned. I had a good run or something. I wonder what Mary and the girls will put on my tombstone. *Here lies a man, or something. He tried, or something.*

As my eyes close, my brain decides to begin bringing systems off-line. My final decommissioning has started. I don't mind too much. Fighting seems like so much work. What's the point? It's just better for everyone that I go with the flow.

Goodnight smell.

Goodbye sight.

Hardly knew ya' touch.

So long, humanity, you were nothing if not a hindrance.

Ahhh ...

Something is happening. What the fuck is that? My black jello starts pulsating around me, interrupting my slumber. I'll ignore it. Go away.

The vibration picks up steam, asserting itself. My little jello-mold, fellow-bold, is falling apart, becoming thin and stretched as the blackness quakes and pulses.

Tears develop then rip wider as bright light streams through. I cling to the pieces but they fall through my fingers. My systems have no choice but to respond to this intrusion and begin coming back online.

As I'm birthed back into the world, I open my eyes in horror with naked anger at the brightness to find myself on my back staring straight up. At first my eyes resist, then grudgingly adjust to the horrible light. Kurt's dumb face is looking down at me. Blinking, I roll over and inventory my left hand. It's charred and scabbed, blood still seeping out of the nubs where my fingers used to be.

I roll back and look up at him. "Why?" I ask.

Kurt rolls the question around in his mouth, tastes it, looks away and then spits back towards me. "My heart is broke, but I have some glue. Help me inhale and mend it with you." His eyes swim with insanity. He points back at something over my head.

I roll over onto my stomach and follow his finger. It's my house. The bright light is the floodlight from my garage. The busted-up bike leans against it. He brought me home.

I plant my hand on the ground and try to clamber to my feet. The pain is immediate and blinding. Lightning bolts shoot up my forearm into my body and then down my legs collapsing them. The fall is short but I absorb it entirely on my chin. My front teeth clip and grind uncomfortably. Pushing up on my elbows, I spit two shattered white chicklets onto the ground. The blood begins spurting up out of my hand again, quickly running down my wrist and puddling on the driveway. My head swoons as my brain loses more critical resources.

The sand is quickly running out of my hourglass. It's about two-hundred feet to the back porch. The glass to the slider gleams brightly and beckons me.

I take a deep breath and gingerly scrunch forward on my elbows and knees. Progress is slow but this is the best I can manage for mobility. Blood drips steadily from my hand and mouth, tracking my progress across the driveway, into the lawn and up the back steps onto the porch. Breadcrumbs.

I peer through the slider. From my perch, I can see straight through the kitchen into the living room. All the lights are off and the room is dark except for the flickering glow of a TV. From the angle just above the floor, I can see Mary under a blanket on the couch. Philly and Ollie are curled up with their own blankets, heads on her lap, asleep. Mary's head is resting on the back of the couch pointed straight up at the ceiling, also asleep.

Lying on my stomach, bleeding, I watch all three blankets move gently up and down as the three women in my life breathe in unison. They look so peaceful and loved.

Something is happening to my face. It purses tightly and then tears start falling thickly out of my eyes, mixing with the blood on my chin, expanding the gore that is pooling in front of me. I wish Mary could see me. Maybe she would forgive me. Maybe my tears are the grease our gears need. Maybe she would look at my pathetic face and decide I have suffered enough, open the kitchen door, and let me crawl back into my house onto the couch and her waiting lap.

The tears pick up as the fantasy cycles through my mind, gaining credibility with each replaying. I raise my bad hand towards the door and scrape the slider quietly with my bloody finger stumps. No one on the couch stirs. I raise the wounded limb higher and sweep it back and forth across the glass. Blood spreads thickly and runs down to the frame. I watch the scene inside through the crimson glaze as my tears increase. I want Mary to look up so badly. I want to take all this back. Seeing them sleeping together on the couch breaks me worse than any homemade pipe bomb could.

With my good hand, I trace "I'm Sorry" into the blood I've smeared on the glass. Peering through the S, I stare at Mary, trying to will her awake. Make the reality you want.

I drum my fingers meekly on the glass, as sobs hiccup violently through my chest. I think it's my imagination at first but it happens again. I'm sure Mary's head bobs. I ramp up the drumming and she stirs a third time. Hope fills my heart as painfully, I make my way to my knees. When she sees me like this, restraining orders, garbage disposals and dead cats will be a thing of the past. I think she sees me.

Suddenly, the carpet is pulled out from under me and my chin scrapes down the glass and bangs off the porch again. It's an earthquake.

Something grabs my ankle wrenching my body away from the door. Mary! I blunt the impact with my good hand as I'm bounced down the stairs by an unknown force, struggling to turn over and confront my tormentor.

Kurt has hold of my left ankle with one hand and with his back to me is dragging my body deeper into the backyard. I kick at him desperately with my right foot but it has no effect. His strength is supernatural.

"Let me go," I yell, between sobs. He doesn't flinch or stop. "I want to go inside. She was going to let me inside. You're ruining everything again." Oblivious to my pleadings, he continues dragging me through the grass.

"Go fuck up your own life and leave me alone," I scream with whatever energy I can muster. Kurt doesn't relent.

He crosses the rest of the yard and dumps me into the sandbox where I buried Friskers. A light switches on in the house as I roll onto my back.

Quietly, patiently Kurt says, "One more special message to

go. And then I'm done, then I can go home."

He raises a shovel over his head and brings it down across my chest. Ribs give way like they're made from paper mâché. Blood spurts out of my mouth and my lungs deflate, but it doesn't really hurt. This is the way it should be. I was fooling myself to think I could ever crawl back under the covers with them. The shovel comes down again and my collarbone disconnects then pops up jaggedly through my skin.

It occurs to me he's aiming for my head but missing. I wonder how many more shots he needs until the shovel finds pay dirt. Ha, "pay dirt," I get it.

He raises it above his head with both hands and lines me up. His eyes are glassy, dead. His feet leave the ground for a moment as he swings the blade down at me. It whistles through the air.

I think about my daughters. About crying while holding them for the first time. Then I think about nothing. Because there is nothing more and that seems like a pretty good way to turn out the lights.

ACKNOWLEDGEMENTS

Thank you to my wife for listening to me talk about useless things for countless hours, while never making them or me seem useless. I'm still unsure of exactly why the universe decided I was worthy of being lucky in this way.

Thank you to my sister, my brothers-in-law Korey and Forrest and to my oldest friend Tyler for reading my first draft and finding humor and substance. I've often turned back to those words of encouragement as both a shield and a balm. Without their support, I wouldn't have found the gumption to follow through. If *Dead Cats,* shocked or offended you, those four share equal blame. Careful Googling may help tell you where to appropriately direct any venom.

Thank you to my Dad for passing on the love of music and sick sense of humor that drives most of the narrative in this book.

Justin, Mike, Isaac – thank you for investing the time to read this and give me valuable feedback.

Lisa Akoury-Ross at SDP Publishing, thank you for all your help navigating through this process.

ABOUT THE AUTHOR

Jesse McKinnell grew up in Massachusetts but moved to Maine as soon as he knew better. On July 4th, 2015, he had a dream about a dentist with a passion for writing sitcoms. Somehow, *Dead Cats and Other Reflections on Parenthood* was the result. It is his first novel. Learn more at jessemckinnell.com or follow him on the Twitters @JesseMcKinnell.

Made in the USA
Middletown, DE
09 May 2018